"P... hands," Longarm ordered quietly.

"Who the hell are you?"

"I'm a United States marshal and I am arresting you."

A voice from across the room bellowed, "That's the big son of a bitch that tossed us out of our house today!"

Longarm saw Willard jump up from a card table in the far end of the room. Suddenly, everything was moving fast. Behind him, Zeke cursed and shoved Longarm aside as he drew his pistol and opened fire on the Wittman brothers.

The room exploded in gunfire. Zeke had knocked Longarm off balance, and he staggered but was able to right his balance and go for his gun. The brothers were fast, but Longarm wasn't where they expected and that gave him a split second's edge. He fired as rapidly as he could pull his trigger.

Men shouted and dived under tables. Willard came crashing through the crowd and Zeke shot him in the belly twice while taking fire. Longarm felt a bullet slice across his shoulder and he emptied his pistol until the Wittman brothers were on the floor.

Willard was screaming and thrashing around in the sawdust and Longarm scooped up the man's gun.

"Nobody move!" he yelled at the top of his voice. "This fight is finished!"

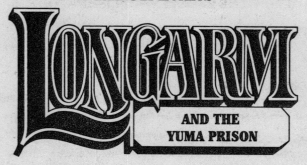

LONGARM

AND THE
YUMA PRISON

JOVE BOOKS, NEW YORK

THE BERKLEY PUBLISHING GROUP
Published by the Penguin Group
Penguin Group (USA) LLC
375 Hudson Street, New York, New York 10014

USA • Canada • UK • Ireland • Australia • New Zealand • India • South Africa • China

penguin.com

A Penguin Random House Company

LONGARM AND THE YUMA PRISON

A Jove Book / published by arrangement with the author

For information, address: The Berkley Publishing Group,
a division of Penguin Group (USA) LLC,
375 Hudson Street, New York, New York 10014.

ISBN: 978-0-515-15433-7

PUBLISHING HISTORY
Jove mass-market edition / April 2014

PRINTED IN THE UNITED STATES OF AMERICA

10 9 8 7 6 5 4 3 2 1

Cover illustration by Milo Sinovcic.

Chapter 1

Deputy United States Marshal Custis Long wished everyone a happy weekend, then stepped outside the Federal Building in downtown Denver. It was Friday and a perfect June afternoon to go to the horse races, have a good meal, and maybe play a few games of poker. At the moment, there was no particular woman in his life and while that was unusual, it also presented him many opportunities. There was, for example, Millie O'Rourke, a fetching waitress and Irish lass who had been giving him the coquettish glances and dropping hints that she would like to become better acquainted. But Longarm had his eye on a young seamstress named Ann who had repaired a small tear in his coat and had made it plain that she wanted to be invited out to dinner . . . and much more.

Longarm tipped his hat at a pretty blond who passed and just as he was about to speak to her, a tall gentleman hurried across the street and kissed the woman on the cheek before taking her arm and leading her away, both of them laughing.

"So," a voice behind him said, "do you have any plans for this weekend?"

Longarm turned to see his boss and good friend, Marshal Billy Vail. "I'm going to the horse races this evening."

"Why don't you come have dinner with me and my family instead? We can have a couple of drinks and . . ."

Longarm thought the world of Billy, but he was of the opinion that Billy's wife was a whiner and his children were noisy and irritating. Not that it wasn't a nice family, but a complaining wife and three boisterous boys were not what he considered to be enjoyable company.

"Thanks for the offer, Billy, but I think I'll pass."

"You always say that. One of these days I'm going to decide that you don't enjoy my wife's cooking."

"Oh, she's a great cook," Longarm lied. "And it's no wonder you've put on quite a lot of weight over the past few years."

Billy patted his small potbelly. "Yes, it's hard to stay in shape, and now that I'm a paper-pushing bureaucrat it gets harder all the time. But my field days are over and I've had a good run. Besides, I needed the promotion because it's not cheap to raise a family."

"I'm sure that's true."

Billy clapped Longarm on the shoulder and said, "It's pot roast and apple pie for dessert if you change your mind. Dinner at seven."

"Thanks," Longarm said, "but another time."

"Have a nice weekend, Custis. One of these days we'll have to get together and go fishing."

"Sure thing." Longarm waved as his friend left, wondering where in the world Billy had ever gotten the idea that he liked to fish.

Longarm descended the steps and started up the street, thinking he'd stop into the Emerald Pub and have a couple of drinks before heading for the local racetrack. But before he had gone even half a block, someone tugged urgently at his sleeve and whispered, "Marshal Custis Long?"

He turned to behold a tall and slender woman in her early twenties with intense dark eyes and wisps of black hair poking out from under a dirty man's cap. She was poorly dressed and although very attractive, he immediately sensed in her an air of real desperation.

"You *are* Custis Long, are you not?"

"Who are you?"

"My name is Jessica Ray."

"Have we met before?"

"No." She paused. "But you knew my father. He was a federal marshal in charge of the same department that you work for."

"You're Tom Ray's daughter?"

She blinked hard, eyelashes wet with tears. "Yes."

"Your father was a legendary lawman and I'm sorry that he was leaving just as I was hired. I hardly knew him, but I remember that he was ambushed and shot up pretty badly and had to retire earlier than he'd planned."

"Father was severely wounded. Shot three times and he should have died of his wounds, but he recovered. It happened when we were together returning from a few days of vacationing up in the mountains."

Longarm's brow furrowed. "That's right. Your mother was killed outright when your buggy left a steep, winding road and rolled down into a canyon."

"I was tossed into the air and suffered a concussion after landing on some rocks. My father was trying to reach me

when someone began shooting from up on the road. My
mother was crushed by the tumbling buggy."

"It was a miracle any of you survived."

"I know."

"I'm really sorry about what happened. I remember that
my current boss, Billy Vail, finally brought the ambusher to
justice. He was sentenced and hanged not long afterward."

"That's right."

Longarm took the young woman's arm. "I was going to
have a few drinks, but now I think I've decided to get something to eat. Would you be kind enough to join me?"

She nodded. "I . . . I didn't stop you just now hoping for
a meal, although I have to admit that I haven't eaten all that
well since arriving in Denver two days ago. Do you have a
wife and family that are expecting you?"

"I'm not married. Jessica, where did you come from and
where is your father?"

"It's a sad and complicated story, Marshal Long, and one
I'd rather not tell you here on the street."

"Then let's find a quiet place to share a good meal. Are
you old enough to have a glass of whiskey or beer?"

"I'm twenty-six and I've shared many a glass with my
father when we were prospecting in the deserts of south-
western Arizona. And then when we struck . . ." Jessica
paused. "Let's just go where we can talk privately."

"How does a big, juicy steak sound?" Longarm asked as
they walked along Colfax Avenue.

"It sounds expensive, but I'm not turning it down . . . if
that is an offer."

"It is," Longarm told her. "So you've only been back to
Denver for a couple of days?"

"That's right. My father and I left here eight years ago.

The town has grown and changed a great deal. There are so many more people on the streets than what I remembered."

"Denver is prospering. But why did you come back?"

"To sell our house."

They entered a nice steak house and Longarm pointed to a corner table in the back where they could speak without being overheard. "Waiter, I'll have a whiskey."

The man looked to Jessica. "I'll have the same."

When they were alone again, Longarm turned his full attention to the young woman. "So you and your father have a house in Denver?"

"That's right. When we left we rented it out. My uncle, Willard Paxton, collected the rent money and took ten percent, which was for his trouble and making sure that all the repairs were made. He managed the rental, but about six months ago, he wrote us in Arizona and said it had burned down. As you might expect, this was a terrible blow to my father because we were prospecting in Arizona and that was our only steady income."

"I see."

Jessica Ray leaned forward. "But the house *didn't* burn down! When I got here that is the first place I visited and guess who was living there?"

"Your uncle?"

"That's right. He and his older brothers, Clyde and Herman."

"You must have had quite a shock."

"I did," Jessica replied in a small voice. "I asked my uncle Willard why he had lied about the house burning down and he said that I must have misunderstood his letter. And then when I said that if that was the case, why weren't we getting any more rent money?"

"Good question."

"My uncle said that my father had deeded over the house to him. But, Marshal, I know that's a lie!"

"Did your uncle offer to show you any papers to prove his claim?"

"He said that there were papers but that they were in the hands of his attorney."

"Whose name is?"

"Lee Monroe."

"I know him," Longarm said. "He is a sleazy man who would rob his own mother of her last dollar. But he has become successful, and I know he has many important clients."

"Then I'm really up against it," Jessica said quietly. "Because I don't have any money to oppose him."

"Maybe I can help. I have a few friends in town that practice law. A couple of them even owe me favors."

Jessica brightened. "Do you . . ."

"Let's talk some more," Longarm urged. "I want to hear the full story before I make a judgment."

Their drinks arrived and they ordered steaks: Longarm preferred his rare; Jessica liked her steak cooked well done. Alone again, Jessica raised her glass. "To justice."

"To justice," Longarm repeated. "So you found me to ask if I'd help you straighten things out with your uncle Willard Paxton and his brothers?"

"Yes . . . and my father."

Longarm frowned. "Let's stick with Uncle Willard for a few more minutes until I understand this completely. Is there any chance that your father deeded over the house to him without telling you?"

"None at all," Jessica replied. "The house was our 'hole

card,' if you will. It was the only thing we had that was worth anything. My father always said that if we never found gold in Arizona, we could at least come back to Denver and have a roof over our heads. And there was that rent money that we relied on. Prospecting, as I'm sure you know, is always a long shot . . . especially in Arizona where everything is so dry and rocky."

"What does your uncle and his brothers do for a living?"

"I have no idea. They used to farm out in eastern Colorado, but my father said they were all lazy and would never make a go of anything requiring hard work."

Longarm removed a pencil from his coat pocket and piece of paper. "What is the address of your house?"

"Four-oh-three Plum Street."

"Nice neighborhood. Does the house look in good repair?"

"It's run-down now and needs paint and the gate is falling over. When Mother was alive she had a rose garden that was the envy of our neighborhood. Now, it's all dead. There are piles of trash in the yard and it looks sad and neglected."

"I'll take a look at it tomorrow," Longarm promised. "Now you said you also needed help for your father. What happened? Did he have an accident while you were prospecting?"

Jessica drained her glass and cleared her throat. "This is hard to tell you, Marshal."

"Just tell me straight out."

She raised her eyes to look into him. "My father shot two men in a Yuma saloon and has been sentenced to life in prison."

It was Longarm's turn to drain his glass. He signaled the waiter for two more drinks and when the man arrived at their table, he said, "Hold the steaks and bring us a bottle of wine with them in about ten minutes."

"Yes, sir."

Longarm leaned back in his chair and studied the young woman closely. "What happened in the Yuma saloon?"

"I was in town shopping for supplies. My father went to the saloon for a few beers. A short time later, I heard gunfire and ran to the saloon. Father had been winged in the arm and two men were lying facedown on the sawdust floor, both dead."

"Had they drawn their guns?"

"I didn't see any guns in their hands, but the sawdust was deep and everyone had crowded around them."

"So what happened next?"

"I rushed to my father's side, and the next thing I knew a big marshal was crashing through the room and pistol-whipped my father, who had slumped back down in a chair. They took him to jail and he was sentenced to the penitentiary a week later."

"Did your father claim self-defense?"

"Yes." Jessica reached across the table and took Longarm's hand, squeezing it hard. "My father is a fine and decent man! He would never just shoot anyone without a good reason."

"Did you visit with him in the jail?"

"Of course. Father said that he was playing poker with the two men. In no time at all, he saw that while they were *pretending* to be strangers to each other, they were really working a crooked deck to cheat him out of his money. When he confronted them, they went for their guns and he was faster and shot straighter."

"Is that what his lawyer told the judge and jury?"

"We didn't have any money for a lawyer. Father spoke in his own defense, and of course, he wasn't very good at it and was sentenced to life in prison." Jessica shook her head. "Father told me to come here and sell the house and use a small part of it to pay a good Yuma lawyer. He said that if his sentence stood, I should take the rest of the money, go far away to a new place, and start my life over without him."

"Weren't there any witnesses in the saloon willing to testify that your father drew and fired in self-defense?"

"There were witnesses," Jessica said bitterly. "But they were friends of the owner and he was friends with the dead men. Justice was never served."

Longarm reached for the fresh glass of whiskey that the waiter delivered and tossed it down. "Bring the wine."

The waiter shrugged as if he didn't care and was gone.

"I'm so sorry to have to burden you with all this trouble," Jessica said. "But my father believes that the two men he killed in that saloon had been paid by Uncle Willard to start a fight and kill him."

"Had you ever seen the two before?"

"No."

"Jessica, I think this is going to be a tough one."

"But will you at least try and get our house back so that I can return to Yuma and hire a lawyer?"

"Yes," he replied. "That I'll do starting tomorrow morning."

"Thank you!"

"You're welcome." Longarm saw that their steaks were on the way. "Let's eat and talk some more. Where are you staying tonight?"

"I . . . I don't have enough money for a room so I was going to see if I could stay . . ."

"You can stay with me, Jessica."

She looked deeply into his eyes. "Marshal, I don't . . ."

"Stop. You can stay and have no fear that I'll force myself upon you. I give you my word as a gentleman."

"All right," she said. "I'll accept your word."

"Let's eat and get a little drunk," he suggested. "And maybe you can tell me something about yourself that brings a smile to my face."

She laughed. "Well, for starters I'm not a virgin."

"Now that *does* put a smile on my face."

"But I'm not greatly experienced with men, either."

Longarm dug into his rare steak, thinking that it might be a long weekend and he wouldn't be going to the racetrack.

Chapter 2

"Nice place you have here," Jessica said, looking around. "Have you lived here long?"

"Two years. It's centrally located near my office and the things I need and most enjoy." Longarm studied Jessica. "Do you have any fresh clothes?"

"No." She looked down at her dirty and baggy men's clothing. "I suppose I should have bought something when I arrived in Denver, but after Uncle Willard sent me packing I was worried about every penny and . . ."

"We'll get you something decent to wear tomorrow morning," Longarm promised. "But for tonight there is a bath down at the end of the hallway and you'll have hot water and I have soap. I'll give you some of my clean clothes to wear tonight."

"I'll look lost and ridiculous in your shirt and pants."

"But you'll be clean and comfortable." Longarm pointed to a big leather couch. "I have extra blankets and a pillow. You'll be fine tonight."

"You're very kind."

"And you and your father are in quite a pickle," Longarm said, removing his flat-brimmed hat and tan coat before unbuckling his cartridge belt.

"How come you wear your sidearm butt forward?"

Longarm shrugged. "It just suits me better." He unbuttoned his vest and showed her the .45-caliber derringer attached to his watch fob.

"Very clever," Jessica said, showing him the small revolver that she carried in her pants pocket.

"Can you hit anything with that little pistol?"

"I'm a pretty decent shot," Jessica replied. "But I'm a lot better with a Winchester rifle."

Longarm found her clean clothes. He rolled up the sleeves to a shirt and also the pants legs. "You're not going to make any fashion statement tonight, but you'll be comfortable and feel better after a hot bath."

"Thanks," she said, accepting the clothes, a towel, and a bar of soap. "Just point me in the right direction."

He opened his door and pointed her down the hallway. "Take your time and enjoy the bath."

"I haven't had a real one with hot water in months," she confessed. "This is going to feel wonderful."

"I'm sure it will. Just knock twice when you're back and I'll unlock the door."

"You keep your door locked even for a little while?"

"Always," he told her. "When you've killed and arrested as many men as your father or I have, you learn to never leave your door unlocked or your back to a crowd."

"Yeah, that's the way Father feels, too."

Longarm must have dozed off in his comfortable chair because he was startled when Jessica knocked twice. He jumped up and opened the door to see her standing bare-footed in the hallway with a smile on her pretty face and his clothes hanging all over her. She had washed her long, black hair and it hung damply over her shoulders all the way down to the prominent swell of her breasts.

"I must look ridiculous," she said, coming into the room. "But I feel much better although I'm a little tipsy from the whiskey and the wine."

"We had a fine meal and a lot to talk about."

"If I ever get our house back and can sell it, I'll take you out to dinner," she promised. "But right now I have less than ten dollars to my name."

"Don't worry about it. Would you like to share a little glass of brandy before we go to bed?"

"As long as it is a *little* glass. Sure, I might as well live it up while I have the chance. I don't even think I've tasted brandy before."

"It's a fine nightcap," Longarm said, pouring them each a small glass. "Here's to getting your house on Plum Street back and your innocent father out of the Yuma Territorial Prison."

"Hear, hear!" she said, smiling broadly. "And here is to you coming with me back to Arizona and helping me get our mining claim back and then us striking it rich."

"You lost your mining claim?"

"Yes, I'm sure it's been taken over. Father and I were always able to find enough gold to keep us going and every-one knows where it is located. As soon as Father was arrested and sent to prison, I had men coming there trying to take it away from me. Some were smooth and promised to help me work it for a share . . . others tried to bully or bed me. One man proposed marriage and another just told me he'd kill me from ambush if I didn't leave."

"But you must have a legal claim."

"It's legal all right, but if you're not there to defend what is yours, then the claim jumpers are on it faster than ants on sugar. My father and I have forty acres of deeded land right up against the Colorado River, north of the penitentiary. Even if there wasn't any gold to be found, just the fact that the claim is beside the river means it has value."

Longarm handed her a glass of brandy. "To better days."

"To better days," she agreed. "And if you help me, I'll make sure that you are fully repaid. I'm sure my father would agree to give you an equal share in our land and mine."

Longarm had no desire to work a hard-rock mining claim . . . even one that promised a fortune in gold. He'd been down near the Arizona border with Mexico more times than he cared to remember. It was an unforgiving country where the summer heat was unbearable and everything either bit, stung, or burned. No, sir, he'd stay far north of Yuma, thank you very much.

"I got you some blankets and that pillow," he said, pointing to the couch.

"Thanks."

He tossed down his brandy. "It's late and we've got a big day ahead of us tomorrow. I think we'd better get to sleep."

"You're right."

Longarm came to his feet and ambled toward his bedroom, removing his pants and shirt. He wasn't sure how this was all going to turn out, but he felt that he would need some help—that meant he'd go see the local sheriff and have either him or one of his experienced deputies go with him when he visited Uncle Willard and his brothers over on Plum Street. Not that he couldn't handle it himself, but with a local lawman, it would make things cleaner and easier.

Local law officials did not appreciate it when a federal officer started pushing his weight around in town. Longarm had learned that the hard way many years ago, and he was taking no chances that something really bad could go wrong and he might have to pull a gun on Jessica's uncle and his brothers. Then again, maybe Jessica's father had signed some papers that had allowed Willard and his brothers to take it over legally and never had gotten around to telling his daughter.

Tomorrow. Tomorrow he would see.

"Sleep late if you can!" Longarm called from his bed into his front room. "We'll have a good breakfast, buy you some clothes, and then set about taking care of business."

"Thank you."

Longarm opened his eyes. He could see Jessica's silhouette standing in his doorway and she was naked. "I thought you were sleepy and worn out."

"I am," she said. "But not *that* sleepy or worn out. I thought you deserved to be thanked for all you've done for me and intend to do."

"There are no strings attached," Longarm told her. "Your father was well respected as an outstanding lawman. I'm helping you out of respect for what he did and because you seem like you really could use a friend here in Denver."

"I could," Jessica said, walking slowly across his bedroom and slipping under the covers to press close to his body. "And I could use a little love if you have it in you."

"I have it in me," he said, taking her into his arms. "But don't do this because . . ."

Jessica Ray didn't let him finish. She pressed her lips onto his and then she spread her legs and opened herself wide. "Don't you think we've already talked enough?"

"I do," he said, feeling an instant and overpowering desire fill his loins and stiffen his rod. Longarm entered Jessica slowly, gently. She smelled clean and wholesome and her body was still damp everywhere.

"Oh, my," she breathed into his ear. "You're the biggest man I've ever had."

"You probably say that to all of them."

"All two others," she whispered in his ear.

He lifted up above her. "You've only had two other men?"

"Actually, one was an older man and the other little more than a sweet boy." Jessica wrapped her legs around Longarm and her hips began to undulate. "So, in a way, you're my first *real* lover. Is that making you excited?"

"I was excited the minute I saw you standing naked in my bedroom door," Longarm grunted as he began to make the bed squeak. "And I think you and I are going to have one hell of an eventful weekend."

"Sounds wonderful to me," she panted, biting his ear. "Now come on and let's see what you've got, big boy."

Longarm showed her what he had and Jessica must have been happy with it because he had to clamp his hand over her mouth to keep her from waking up the entire second floor of his living quarters.

Chapter 3

"Well," the lady at the dress shop mused, sizing Jessica up in her baggy men's clothes. "I think I can make quite a difference in your appearance. I have several dresses that I believe were made for your slender figure."

"One dress is enough," Jessica said. "I don't want to take advantage of my new friend's generosity."

The woman glanced out toward Longarm, who was standing on the boardwalk waiting. "I have a feeling that he might be taking advantage of you, young lady."

"No, ma'am! He's doing this out of respect for my father."

"Oh, really?" she asked, eyebrows lifting. "And not because you are a very pretty young woman who is extremely grateful?"

Jessica blushed. "I'm no angel," she confessed. "And I never pretended to be any better or worse than most. But if you'll just show me an inexpensive dress, I'd be happy."

"And you'll need some new undergarments, I'm sure."

Again, Jessica blushed. "I suppose so."

"And you can't be wearing those old work boots with a new dress and bonnet."

"I suppose not, but . . ."

"I'll bet you wear the same size shoe as I do," the woman said, gazing down at the old work boots on Jessica's feet. "And you know what?"

"What?"

"I have a few extra pairs that I never wear and I'm just sure that they would look far better on you than they do on me."

"I . . . I don't know."

"I *do* know. You see, young lady, I take great pride in my clothing and I couldn't imagine sending you out of my shop wearing a lovely dress that perfectly fits you but you having on those awful, dirty old boots." She waved her hands about her head. "It would be like . . . like looking at a classic Roman marble sculpture wearing work boots!"

"I've never seen a Roman sculpture," Jessica admitted.

"Well, I've never seen one in real life, but I've seen pictures of a few and I assure you that they wouldn't wear old work boots." The dress shop owner looked past Jessica to study Longarm again. "He's a famous United States marshal, isn't he?"

"Yes."

"Probably in his mid-thirties, handsome and tall, but worn from danger."

"He's a good man and he's going to help me."

"And you are how old, my dear?"

"I'm in my twenties, ma'am." Jessica didn't like the way that this conversation was going. "I'm a fully grown woman who doesn't need to be lectured. Now, do you have something inexpensive that I can wear, or should I go somewhere else to do my shopping?"

"I have what you need," the woman said, her expression softening. "And forgive me if I've been too forward. It's just that Marshal Custis Long has quite a reputation here in Denver with the ladies and you seem a little . . . uh, naïve. I don't want you to be hurt or taken advantage of, that's all."

"I understand and appreciate your concern. But I know what I'm doing and I'm not all that naïve. I've seen the hard side of life, ma'am. I can take care of myself when I have to."

"Glad to hear that. So let's see what we have that you'll look good in and won't cost the marshal a month's pay."

Longarm hardly recognized Jessica when she finally exited the shop wearing a beautiful blue dress with white lace around the hem and wrists. She also was wearing a pair of new shoes and a fetching sun bonnet.

"My, oh, my," Longarm exclaimed. "I'm going to have to beat the men off you with a club!"

Her eyes danced. "Do I *really* look pretty now?"

"Very pretty!" And it was true. Not only had the woman in the dress shop found Jessica a lovely dress, but she also had given her an air of self-confidence that had previously been lacking. "Take my arm, Miss Ray, and we'll stroll a bit around the town."

"I'd be most proud to do so," she said. "But I thought we were going to go see the local sheriff and then confront Uncle Willard and his brothers about my house."

"All business this morning, huh?"

"I'm sorry, Custis. But every day that my father suffers in the Yuma prison is a day that he can't reclaim and I can't enjoy. I . . . I wish that I could, but I need to resolve this house business and return to Arizona with enough money to try and hire a lawyer who will set my father free."

"And then you'll have to fight to retake your mining claim."

"There is no doubt about that," Jessica said. "And that's not going to be easy or safe." She looked up into his eyes. "I meant what I said last night about us giving you an equal share . . . if only you'll help us."

His smile faded. "Jessica, I . . ."

She placed a finger over his lips. "Don't say anything, Custis. Please don't make your decision yet. Help me get the house back so I'll have some money and then I can pay you if . . ."

Longarm bent over and kissed her hard. It wasn't something that he had planned or even thought that he wanted to do, but the feeling had suddenly come upon him and he didn't care if people on this busy street were watching. There was just something about Jessica Ray, a terrible vulnerability, a great trust that she had in him and her courage to do whatever it took to free her father and regain her mining claim that made him think she was very, very special. Also, she had made love so desperately, so inexpertly but passionately the night before in his bed that he couldn't shake the memory from his mind.

"Help me, please," she whispered. "If you can't come to Arizona, I'll understand. But if I don't at least get our house back and sold, there is nothing at all I can do for Father."

"I'm going to help you, Jessica. Don't you doubt that for even a moment."

"Uncle Willard has killed a man. His brothers are lazy and piggish, but they are not cowards. When we get to Plum Street, the house is going to look terrible, but if I have a few days to clean inside and maybe a small loan from you to get it repainted and fixed up just a little bit, I just know it will sell quickly and for at least a few thousand dollars."

"Probably more," Longarm heard himself say. "It's a very desirable neighborhood and yours is the only house on the block that looks like hell."

"It can look nice again. I just need a little time, loan, and help."

"Don't you think that we've talked enough already?"

Jessica laughed. "That was my line last night just before I hopped into your bed and we made love."

"Yeah, it was. Now let's go to the sheriff's office and see if anyone is in and if they want to accompany us to your house."

"Okay." She patted her hip. "I made sure that this new dress you bought for me has pockets and I've got my little pistol ready just in case we have to fight it out with bullets."

"Did that dress shop owner see your pistol?"

"Yes."

"Well," Longarm added, "what did she say?"

"She said that as pretty as I was going to look in this new dress I needed one and that I should not hesitate to use it if you or any other man tried to take advantage of me."

Longarm let out a guffaw. "Well, I'll have to remember that, Miss Ray."

She squeezed his arm. "You can take advantage of me any old time you feel like it, Custis."

"How about tonight?"

"Assuming we won't get shot to death, I'd be disappointed if you waited any longer."

"Jessica," Longarm muttered. "If you keep talking like that I might lose my head and follow you all the way to Yuma."

"Actually, I'm already counting on it."

"I have a job here in Denver."

"Take some time off," she told him. "Stick with me all the way and help my father; you'll be rewarded like a king."

"With gold."

"And more," she whispered, giving him a seductive wink while dropping her hand to slip it down the inside of his leg.

Longarm grinned broadly and felt his manhood stiffen as they walked close together down the street.

Chapter 4

It was easy enough to find the sheriff's office, but when they arrived, there was an old man sitting at a desk smoking a briar pipe and reading the newspaper. He glanced over his paper at Longarm and Jessica, then turned his attention back to the newspaper, saying, "If you're lookin' for Sheriff Morrell, you'll find him over at the hospital. I don't expect him to show up for a few days and I'm just watching over things here."

Longarm approached the old man and said, "Are you a deputy?"

"No, I'm Art Morrell's father, Zeke Morrell. My son tried to break up a saloon fight last night and someone hit him over the back of his head with a chair. Once he was down, a pair of brothers kicked the hell out of him. He's laid up at the hospital."

"I'm sorry to hear that."

Zeke laid the paper down. There were dark circles around his eyes and he looked exhausted. "Who are you folks and how can I help you?"

"I'm a deputy United States marshal named Custis Long. I usually go to the main office, but we're out in this part of town and I wanted to stop by and inform the sheriff here that we have a problem with some men who have illegally taken over this lady's home."

"I can't help you with that, Marshal, and I doubt that my son could help you, either. It sounds to me like you need an attorney, not a sheriff."

"That might be true, but we're going over to the house in question to try to get some answers. I was just stopping by out of professional courtesy."

"I'm sure my son would have appreciated that," Zeke said, coming to his feet and extending his hand. "But my son is in pretty bad shape. There are two brothers named Pace and Slade Wittman and they're the ones that sent my son to the hospital. I don't suppose you'd be willing to arrest and bring them back to this jail?"

"Doesn't your son have any deputies?"

"Nope. We're unincorporated here and underfunded."

Longarm scowled. It was not unusual for small localities in the suburbs of big towns to have their own staffs rather than rely on Denver to handle their issues. The trouble was, those localities, while adamant about retaining their independence, usually were poorly run and perpetually out of money.

"I can check into the matter," Longarm offered. "But for the time being I need to help this young lady, Miss Jessica Ray."

The old man smiled. "I sure don't blame you for putting my boy on the back burner given how pretty she is. I'd go after Pace and Slade myself except they'd either shoot or beat the shit out of me. I'm too old and slow to take on a young and dangerous pair like that."

"What did they do that had your son trying to arrest them?"

"They beat up a whore a few days ago. Almost killed her. Her name was Loretta Love . . . probably not her real name . . . and they did some things to her that ought not to happen to an animal. When she fought back, they hurt her so bad that she can't eat or see out of either eye."

Longarm's face tightened. "Where do those sons o' bitches hang out?"

"At the Buffalo Saloon."

"I know where it's at. Maybe I'll pay a visit to them after we get this house trouble settled on Plum Street."

"Nice street," Zeke said. "Houses are expensive there now. More than me or my son could ever afford."

"Do you want to come along and just watch what happens?" Longarm asked. "We could use a witness if things get rough."

"If I do that, would you pay a visit to the Buffalo Saloon and arrest those Wittman brothers and bring them back here so I can lock 'em up in our jail and feed them dog shit and beans, with my piss in their coffee and spit on their breakfast eggs?"

"You'd do that?" Jessica asked with shock.

"I sure would," Zeke said, eyes hard as obsidian. "And when my son gets out of the hospital, they'll get worse until they go before a judge and are sentenced to a prison. Marshal Long, they are too tough for the likes of me . . . but I got a feeling that you could handle them easy enough."

Longarm turned around and studied the front door for a minute. He felt Jessica's hand on his arm and heard her whisper, "It sounds like you need to help this man."

"Yeah, but I need to help you first," Longarm told her. "I can tell you one thing, this weekend sure isn't shaping up to be the relaxing two days that I'd intended it to be."

"Are you sorry we got together?" she asked, closely studying his face.

"No."

"Good!"

"All right," Longarm said, turning around to face the old man. "If you tag along as a witness, I'll drop by the Buffalo Saloon early this evening and put some misery on Pace and Slade Wittman."

"And you'll arrest and bring them here to jail."

"Yeah, I'll do that, too. But you might have to pay for someone to carry them over here because I don't have much use for a woman beater or a couple of men who would kick a lawman when he's down."

Zeke filled his lungs and smiled for the first time. He marched over to the gun rack and found a shotgun and then he checked to make sure that both barrels were loaded. He also snatched a badge off his son's desk and pinned it on his chest. "Let's go!"

Longarm allowed himself a small grin. "Zeke, before we do this we have to have an understanding."

"Which is?"

"I'm in charge and I'll do the talking. You keep that scattergun pointed down at the ground and don't use it unless it's absolutely necessary and bullets are being fired."

"You've my word on that." He turned to Jessica. "Miss, why don't you just stay here at the office and make yourself comfortable?"

"Why don't you button up your fly before you expose and embarrass yourself?"

Zeke grabbed at his crotch, discovered that his fly was open and that his little wiener was poking out like a worm from its hole. The man colored and turned away suddenly.

"Gawdamn old age," he muttered. "A man hits seventy and he loses all his dignity and good sense. Can't remember anything and just generally is pathetic."

"Don't be so hard on yourself," Longarm told the man. "In your day I'll bet you were quite a fine figure of manhood."

"I was! But that day is long gone and look at me now. Not even enough gumption and fire in my belly to go over to the Buffalo Saloon on my own tonight and take on the Wittman brothers for beating a whore and my son half to death."

"I'll make it right by you and your son," Longarm promised.

"And I'll be there to back you up," Zeke promised.

"Me, too," Jessica added. "We're going to make a good team and we'll soon cut our teeth on my Uncle Willard and his two brothers."

Zeke's eyes widened. "Did your own uncles really steal your house?"

"Yes."

"That ain't right."

"No," Jessica said, "but just like with the poor woman and your son, we're going to set things straight."

Zeke nodded, screwed down his hat, and followed Jessica and Longarm out the door, carefully locking it in his wake.

Chapter 5

Longarm had often thought that, if he lived to get old and had saved some money, Plum Street would be just about right. All of the houses, while not huge, were well kept as were their yards. They were constructed of red brick and had nice porches. There were flower gardens everywhere and on some of the fences were big roses . . . yellows, whites, reds, and a pretty peach color that was his personal favorite. Being a nice day, many children were out and about playing ball in the street and quite a few families were enjoying their Saturday by sitting on their porch sipping tea and watching the world go by. Denver winters were hard so when the weather was as pleasant as it was today, people liked to stay outdoors.

"That's Uncle Willard and his brothers sitting on our front porch," Jessica said quietly.

"Yeah, I spotted your house the minute we rounded the corner and started up the block. It looks like hell."

"It didn't used to look like that."

The three men were large and slovenly. They were dressed in bib overalls without shirts and when they saw Jessica, two of them jumped up and went into the house to emerge a moment later with guns in their hands. Longarm took this all in without breaking stride.

"Just let me do the talking."

"That's fine with me, but talk won't get them to leave," Jessica replied. "Willard is the biggest one with the red bandanna tied around his throat."

When Longarm came to the sagging front gate, he pushed it aside and took a few steps up the walk. "Afternoon," he said, cheerfully.

"What do you want?" Willard turned a cold stare on Jessica. "If you brought some friends to help you, they aren't enough." He turned his eyes back on Longarm. "I'll thank you to get off our property."

Longarm didn't budge. "I'm assuming your name is Willard and the other two drinking whiskey with one hand and holding pistols in the other are your brothers, Clyde and Herman."

"That's right."

"Miss Ray says that you have no right to live in her house and she wants you to pay her back rent and to get out of the house today."

"Ha! We ain't payin' no back rent and we damn sure ain't leavin'. This here property is ours now."

"I'd like to see the legal papers saying that is the case."

"The papers ain't here."

"Where are they?"

The three men exchanged quick glances and one of them said, "At our lawyer's office. His name is Mr. Lee Monroe."

Longarm nodded and showed them his badge. "Monroe is crooked."

They stared at his badge, unsure what to say or do next. Finally, the one that hadn't spoken yet blurted, "Even the law can't take a man's house."

Longarm pointed down the street. "Do you think your lawyer lives over there?"

All three men pivoted to look just as Longarm expected and when they turned back, Longarm's gun was on them. "You men have no right to be here and you've done considerable damage to this property. Get out of those chairs and come down here right now or I'll come up and drag you off the porch and split your heads open in the process."

"You got no right to do this!"

Zeke cocked back the hammers of his shotgun. "The marshal has given you an order, and you're just lucky we don't arrest you."

"Arrest us!"

"That's right," Longarm said, "and I'm not asking you boys to leave again."

"But . . . but every damn thing we own is inside!" one of the men cried. "We got rifles and stuff worth a lot of money."

"Glad to hear that," Longarm said. "We'll sell it for the damages and back rent you owe Miss Ray. If what you leave behind doesn't cover the charges, where can I find you three deadbeats?"

"Son of a bitch!" Willard wailed. "You'll be hearing from Mr. Monroe about this house!"

"Send him over right away," Longarm told them. "I've met him before and I promise you that he won't be eager to get reacquainted."

Willard's eyes narrowed. "You know him?"

"That's right. I almost got him disbarred last year and I'm betting this time I'll get him run out of town."

The three men swore and stepped down from the porch. "This isn't over," Willard growled as he passed through the gate. "It ain't over by a long shot."

Zeke jammed his shotgun into the man's gut. "Maybe you want it to end right now. Huh?"

The blood drained out of Willard's round face and he backpedaled so fast he tripped over a trash can and went sprawling. His brothers picked him up and they set off down the street cussing and screaming at the top of their lungs. Several of the neighbors who were sitting on their front porches began to clap and jeer the brothers.

Jessica rushed inside, stopped in her tracks, and breathed, "Oh my God, it's even worse than I'd feared."

Longarm and Zeke were right behind her and they immediately saw what she meant. The interior of the house was a disaster. It stunk from garbage laying on kitchen counters and on tables littered with cigarette butts and dirty dishes.

"I want to cry," Jessica wailed. "It's awful!"

Zeke walked over and inspected a good Winchester rifle. In a pair of saddlebags he found some money and slowly counted it out after clearing a table of refuse. "Comes to almost two hundred dollars."

"It'll have to do," Longarm said. "We'll hire a couple of people to start cleaning. Jessica, this house will be looking good inside just a few days."

"I'll believe that when I see it," she replied, grabbing a broom and starting to work. "What pigs!"

Longarm and Zeke found some trash cans and began helping. Longarm wasn't happy about any of this, but he figured

Jessica was worth the trouble, and although he'd lied to the brothers about nearly running attorney Monroe out of Denver, he hadn't lied about the man's sleazy and unethical reputation. If Monroe had a document, it would be forged and that would be his undoing.

As if reading his mind, Zeke said, "You think that their attorney will show up pretty quick?"

"No," Longarm said. "I don't. When Willard and his brothers run to him and tell the man who I am, he'll know better than to push things. My guess is that he'll tear up any phony documents and we'll never hear a peep out of him."

"Hope you're right."

"Lee Monroe has been tap-dancing with the law for years," Longarm continued. "I've spoken to him a few times and he doesn't want to cross me. I'm almost sure this is over."

"Then that leaves us free to visit the Buffalo Saloon tonight."

"That's right," Longarm agreed, moving outside as Jessica began raising a big cloud of dust with her fast-moving broom. "This is turning out to be a very productive day."

Chapter 6

Longarm and Jessica sat on the front porch of the Plum Street house, sipping coffee and watching the sun go down. They hadn't spoken for a while but had waved at some of the passersby, many with children in tow. Finally, Longarm said, "This is a fine little house. Are you sure you want to sell it?"

"I need the money for that Yuma lawyer," she replied. "And besides, I have memories here of my mother and father and while most are good, the house is haunted with those remembrances. I think I would always feel some loss here."

"Maybe so. You've got quite a bit of work to be done here if you're going to try and sell it."

"I'll go after it hard and maybe I'll find some help," Jessica told him.

"I know a good and honest real estate salesman. Would you like him to stop by and give you some idea of an asking price?"

"Sure. But let's wait on that at least until I've cleaned up the inside and fumigated the place. Can I still spend nights at your place?"

"I'd be disappointed if you didn't."

"What about this business with Zeke and the Buffalo Saloon? Are you going there with him to arrest those brothers that put the sheriff in the hospital this evening?"

"I am," Longarm told her.

"I'll be worried about you."

"I'll be fine. They don't know me and I'll have the advantage of surprise. I'm more worried about Zeke than I am about myself."

"Why?"

"He hates the Wittman brothers, and I'm concerned that he might go off half-cocked and start a shoot-out in the saloon."

"Maybe you should insist that he stays at the jail."

"He wouldn't do that. But I will make him leave his shotgun at the office. The last thing we need is for him to open with both barrels into a small space crowded with people."

"I see what you mean," Jessica said quietly. "I'll be waiting at your place when this is over."

"There is an extra key hidden under the potted plant at the end of the hall," Longarm told her. "Help yourself to whatever you need there."

"I'll be needing you," she told him.

"That's music to my ears, Jessica."

Ten minutes later the sun was down and Longarm was on the move. He stopped by a small café and had a quick meal, then made his way to the sheriff's office to find Zeke pacing the floor with impatience.

"What took you so long?" the man challenged.

"I spent some time with Jessica just watching the folks passing by and then had a meal." Longarm studied the older man. "Look, Zeke, I wish you'd just stay here and let me arrest those brothers."

"You don't even know what they look like."

"I can ask the bartender to point them out . . . hell, they may not even be there this evening."

"They will be there," Zeke said, voice shaking with anger, as he walked over to grab the shotgun.

"That stays here," Longarm told the man.

"The hell you say!"

"Zeke, a shotgun in a saloon shoots too wide a pattern. If you opened it up on the Wittman brothers, you could kill some innocent bystanders and I won't have that."

Zeke glared at Longarm. "I told you that I'm not much good with a pistol anymore. Slow and not all that accurate."

"All the more reason why you should stay here and wait until I bring them in to be jailed."

"I can't do that."

"If you want my help, you'll play by my rules. What's it going to be?"

Zeke's inward struggles showed on his old, lined face but at last he nodded his head. "All right, I'll do it your way."

"When we enter the saloon, point the brothers out to me and stay back. If they see us together, I'll have lost my advantage of surprise. Understand?"

"I understand."

"Then let's go."

Longarm headed outside and took in a deep breath of fresh air. He knew that a rough crowd frequented the Buffalo Saloon and there was a good possibility that a few of them would recognize him as a federal lawman. There might even be a couple of men that he'd arrested and sent to jail or prison. But that could not be helped.

"There it is," Zeke said. "Sounds crowded."

"Yeah," Longarm agreed. "Let's just ease inside nice and quiet. You look around and tell me when you spot the brothers."

"Count on it," Zeke said in a tight voice.

Longarm entered first and the saloon was packed. He stepped aside of the doorway and let Zeke join him. A full minute went by and then Zeke started moving through the noisy crowd. Longarm followed after the old man, ready to grab him by the collar and pull him out of danger.

"There they are," Zeke said much too loudly as he headed straight for the brothers.

The Wittman brothers were twins. They were handsome and not particularly large men and both wore guns on their hips. They were standing together at the far end of the bar laughing and talking to a couple of saloon girls.

Longarm grabbed Zeke by the sleeve and yanked him back. The brothers spotted Zeke and the smiles died on their faces. Something passed between them and they eased away from the bar and suddenly the room was quiet and filled with tension.

Longarm knew that the brothers had seen him grab and pull Zeke aside and now his advantage of surprise was lost.

"You two are under arrest for assaulting and seriously injuring Sheriff Morrell in this saloon. Also, I understand you beat the hell out of a woman who worked here."

"A whore," one of the brothers said, "who got mouthy and got her mouth filled with my fist."

"Put your guns on the bar top and do it with your left hands," Longarm ordered quietly.

"Who the hell are you?"

"I'm a United States marshal and I am arresting you."

A voice from across the room bellowed, "That's the big son of a bitch that tossed us out of our house today!"

Longarm saw Willard jump up from a card table in the far end of the room. Suddenly, everything was moving fast. Behind him, Zeke cursed and shoved Longarm aside as he drew his pistol and opened fire on the Wittman brothers.

The room exploded in gunfire. Zeke had knocked Longarm off balance and he staggered, but was able to right his balance and go for his gun. The brothers were fast, but Longarm wasn't where they expected and that gave him a split second's edge. He fired as rapidly as he could pull his trigger. Men shouted and dived under tables. Willard came crashing through the crowd and Zeke shot him in the belly twice while taking fire. Longarm felt a bullet slice across his shoulder and he emptied his pistol until the Wittman brothers were on the floor. Willard was screaming and thrashing around in the sawdust and Longarm scooped up the man's gun.

"Nobody move!" he yelled at the top of his voice. "This fight is finished!"

Zeke collapsed, arm sweeping mugs of beer from the bar's top as he went down.

Longarm backed up a step, taking everything in with a glance. The room was dead still, most of the customers either streaming out the saloon's rear entrance into an alley or lying frozen on the sawdust.

"Son of a bitch!" Longarm swore, gun still up as he knelt beside Zeke. "You crazy old bastard!"

But Zeke wasn't listening because he was dead. So were the Wittman brothers and big, fat Willard.

Four dead men in four seconds, maybe a few more. Longarm glanced at his shoulder and saw the blood soaking into his coat.

"Are you really a federal marshal," the bartender finally asked, breaking the silence like the shattering of glass.

Longarm nodded and removed his badge. He showed it to the bartender and the rest of the crowd. "Anyone see who shot first?"

"The old man," one of the patrons offered. "He put a slug in Slade Wittman and then Pace put a couple in him and that's all that I saw before all hell broke loose."

Longarm glared at the crowd. He spotted Willard's brothers sitting frozen at their card table and braced them. "If you fat sons o' bitches have a mind to settle a score with me, then stand up and go for your guns right now."

They both wagged their chins back and forth.

Longarm pointed the barrel of Willard's gun first at one and then the other. "You're leaving town and never returning," he told them. "If I see either of you, I'll shoot on sight. Understood?"

They nodded.

"Then get the hell out of Denver."

"Can't we even take Willard to be buried someplace?" one of the brothers whined.

"All right, drag him out of here in a hurry!"

Longarm shoved Willard's gun in behind his belt and picked up his own weapon and holstered it. "We're taking up a collection here tonight. Every man in this room is going to put money into the hat for the burial of Zeke Morrell and the medical expenses of his son, Sheriff Morrell, who was beaten half to death in this saloon.

Longarm picked up Zeke's hat and sent it around the

room. "If I see any man not contributing, I'll deal with him right now!"

The hat filled with greenbacks and coins. It overflowed with money. Longarm shoved it all into his pocket and picked up Zeke's body and left the saloon.

Chapter 7

On Monday morning, Longarm went to his office and sought out his boss, Billy Vail.

"Come on in and close the door," Billy said, looking up from his ever-present pile of paperwork. "You look worn out, Custis. I thought you were planning on going to the horse races and having a quiet time this weekend."

Longarm took a chair. "Well, sometimes our plans just don't work out right. Billy, I hate to tell you this, but I was in a shoot-out at the Buffalo Saloon this weekend."

Billy laid down his pen and stared hard at his deputy marshal. "What the hell happened this time?"

"It's kind of a long story and I don't think it's one that you're going to like."

"I'm sure that it isn't," Billy said. "But tell me anyway."

"Well, Friday when I left here I was sought out by a young lady from Arizona named Miss Jessica Ray."

"Ray," Billy said. "I knew a—"

"It's his daughter," Longarm interrupted.

"Tom Ray's daughter showed up here in Denver after all these years? What happened to her father?"

"He's serving a lifetime sentence in the Yuma penitentiary for murder."

Billy dropped his pen and stared. "Tom was a mighty good man. I can't quite imagine that he'd kill someone without provocation or good reason."

"His daughter says that Tom was playing poker at a saloon in Yuma when he realized that two of the men at the table were working together to rig the game. When he confronted them, the shooting started and Tom was faster and shot straighter. Then, the local marshal barged into the room and pistol-whipped Tom from behind. Tom Ray was hauled up before a judge and sentenced to life in prison."

Billy shook his head. "Surely there must have been witnesses in that saloon willing to testify that Tom Ray shot and killed in self-defense."

"Apparently not." Longarm leaned back in his chair. "Tom and his daughter, Jessica, prospected all over southern Arizona and they finally staked a claim by the Colorado River that was proving to be very profitable. Jessica thinks that the reason why the judge and the marshal railroaded Tom is because they wanted his mining claim."

"I see." Billy shook his head. "Tom left here eight or nine years ago after he and his wife and daughter were ambushed. The wife died and Tom became a very bitter man. I liked him, but he was a powder keg waiting to explode."

"What are you trying to say?" Longarm asked.

"I'm not trying to say anything. But I am suggesting that Tom left Denver an embittered man. He may have taken to hard drinking and fighting. It's possible, Custis, that the two men he shot to death weren't really working together and that they didn't draw their guns first. It's possible that Tom Ray has fallen so low that he gunned down two innocent men and received the proper life sentence."

Longarm considered this for a few moments. "All right," he said, "it is possible that justice was served in Yuma. But what if Jessica Ray is right and that her father was set up to take a murder charge so that he would lose his gold mine?"

"Is his daughter's name on the mining claim they had along the river?"

"I don't know."

"If it isn't, then I'm not sure what you or anyone else can do about this," Billy mused aloud. "And my next question is, why are you getting involved?"

"Because Jessica Ray is being railroaded. Her uncle, Willard Paxton, and his two brothers, Clyde and Herman . . ."

"Wait a minute! What has this uncle to do with Tom Ray and his imprisonment for murder?"

"Like I said, it's a long story. But the short of it is that Zeke Morrell shot and killed . . ."

"Old Zeke Morrell, the former sheriff?"

"Yeah. You see, these two brothers, the Wittmans, got the drop on Zeke's son, Sheriff Art Morrell, and damn near beat him to death . . . along with a saloon whore. So Zeke and I went to the saloon to arrest the brothers."

"Don't tell me," Billy groaned. "There was a gunfight and you shot the brothers to death along with all three of Jessica Ray's uncles."

"No," Longarm said quickly. "I shot one of the Wittman brothers, but old Zeke shot the other along with Willard. I let two of Jessica Ray's uncles leave the saloon but warned them to get out of Denver."

Billy waved his hands in the air. "Hold on! You killed

one of the Wittman brothers, but old Zeke Morrell killed the other and Uncle Willard?"

"That's about the size of it." Longarm sighed. "But Zeke was killed in the battle. I had the crowd take up a collection for him and his son who is in the hospital."

Billy groaned. "I can't believe this," he said. "What a mess!"

"I know," Longarm said, looking a bit chagrined. "But you see, Uncle Willard and his brothers had taken over Jessica's house and—"

"Enough!" Billy cried. "You're giving me a headache!"

"Sorry, Billy, but I told you it was complicated."

Billy placed his head in his hands. "Custis, you should have come over to my house and had some of that pot roast and my wife's apple pie like I begged you to do Friday afternoon."

"Yeah, you're right, Billy."

"So instead you get yourself involved with Tom Ray's daughter and wind up in a big fucking gunfight where old Zeke Morrell, Uncle Willard, and two gawdamn brothers end up dead."

"They had stomped Sheriff Morrell into the sawdust and sent him to the hospital with major injuries," Longarm said. "Are we in the business of letting someone do that to our own kind now?"

"Of course not," Billy snapped. "But you could have waited until this morning and gotten some advice and help."

"Some things don't wait well," Longarm said quietly. "I did take up a collection at the saloon for Zeke and to help pay his son's medical bills. And there are witnesses aplenty that saw how it all happened and that I wasn't the one that drew my gun first."

"You said Zeke did that."

"Well, I'm pretty sure that he did. Actually, there was so much shooting and shoving and all hell breaking loose that it was a little hard to say who did what exactly when."

"Oh, man," Billy moaned. "This day is starting out to be the worst ever."

Longarm came to his feet. "You're taking this a little too hard, Billy. We got Uncle Willard and his brothers out of that house on Plum Street and Jessica is cleaning it up like crazy. She intends to sell the house and use the money for a Yuma lawyer that will get her father out of that penitentiary."

"Okay! Okay!" Billy shouted. "But can you just . . . just let it go and stay out of the entire mess now?"

"Not yet," Longarm said. "I'm going to pay a visit to Lee Monroe, the attorney. Uncle Willard said that he had some papers proving that ownership. Of course, the papers have to be false documents. I need to get that cleared up before Jessica can sell her house."

"So what are you intending to do when you meet the attorney? Shoot him down?"

"Hell no. I'll just put some fear into him and get the matter straightened out right away. Billy, I'm sure you've heard of the man and know that he's as crooked as a dog's back leg."

"Yeah, I've heard that, but I really don't want you to do any more damage than has already been done."

"Sorry, Billy. But I've got to get this deed thing straightened out for Jessica Ray."

"You're screwing her."

Longarm made a face. "Come on! You know that isn't a nice way to put it."

"Nice or not, you're screwing Tom Ray's daughter and she's got you hooked into this all the way. True or not?"

"Okay, we're . . . we're sleeping together."

"No, you're not. If you were sleeping you wouldn't have those dark circles around your eyes. You left here on Friday afternoon looking rested and good. You come into my office on Monday morning, tell me you were involved in a shooting that claimed four lives and you look like hell."

"I just need a good night's sleep, Billy. You don't have to have such a chapped ass over this whole thing. Justice needed to be served this weekend and I just happened to have my name called. You'd have done the same thing given the same circumstances."

"Bullshit!"

Longarm got up and headed for the door. "I hope you make the coffee a little stronger than usual. I'm going to check on things at my desk, have a cup of coffee, and then go see that attorney, Lee Monroe. As soon as I get that settled, I'll get back into a routine."

"I very much doubt that."

"You'll see," Longarm told his boss as he left the office, "I'll just get this last little thing taken care of and then get back to normal."

"Hey!" Billy yelled.

Longarm stopped in the middle of the office. "You don't have to shout, Billy."

"Just don't you even think of going to Yuma, Arizona!"

"Never entered my mind, Boss."

Billy muttered something and slammed his door, causing Longarm to wonder if the man's own weekend had also been a disaster.

Chapter 8

"I can do this alone," Longarm told Jessica. "You don't have to come along."

"I want to meet this despicable man," Jessica insisted. "I want to look him in the eye and tell him he's dishonest and should be disbarred."

"I doubt that you'll hurt his feelings," Longarm told her. "I've seen Lee Monroe in the courtroom a few times and he's both ruthless and arrogant."

"I don't care. Let's pay the man an unexpected visit."

Twenty minutes later they entered Lee Monroe's handsome law office and when Longarm showed the receptionist his federal officer's badge, the woman asked, "May I tell Mr. Monroe what this is about?"

Longarm glanced over her shoulder to a closed door with the attorney's name. "Is he in right now?"

"Yes, but he's with a client. I can't just let you barge in on him right now."

"It's not your choice," Longarm said, taking Jessica's hand and marching past the receptionist to open the door.

The attorney was getting an energetic blow job. The woman who was giving it to Lee Monroe may have been a "client," perhaps working off some of his fees during office hours. When Longarm and Jessica barged in, Monroe was sitting on the edge of his desk and the woman was naked with her face buried in his crotch.

"Holy shit!" Monroe cried in consternation. "What the hell are—"

"Excuse me for interrupting," Longarm said, barely able to hold back a laugh. "But we needed to speak to you right away. However, if you want to let the lady finish up . . . we can wait a minute or two."

The woman was in her forties, not pretty, and a bit on the heavy side. She straightened up fast, ran a forearm across her wet lips, and hissed, "Who are you sons o' bitches?"

"I'm Marshal Custis Long and . . . well, never mind. Are you finished with him or . . ."

"Gawdamn you, Marshal! I'll have your ass for this!" attorney Monroe screamed. "Cynthia!"

The receptionist appeared in the doorway behind Longarm and Jessica. She did not seem particularly surprised to see her boss with his trousers down around his ankles or the flabby woman grabbing her clothing. "Yes, Mr. Monroe?" she said with a smile.

"You're . . . you're *fired*!"

"I was going to quit anyway, you slimy bastard." Cynthia laughed out loud. "This is the best ending I could ever have imagined, asshole."

And then the receptionist turned around and left the office.

"So," Longarm said as Jessica stood at his side with her mouth hanging open. "This is Miss Jessica Ray and I wanted to tell you that we have evicted a Mr. Willard Paxton . . . now deceased . . . and his worthless brothers. But while he was among the living, Willard told us that you have some papers that prove he owns the house on Plum Street. We'd like to see them right now."

Monroe was frantically trying to pull his trousers up, but he was so frustrated that he was having a hell of a time. "You bastard!"

Longarm took two quick strides forward and backhanded the attorney so hard that he slid across his desk and fell on the floor. "Let's see some legal papers," he commanded.

"Fuck you!" Monroe shrieked. "I'll have your asses for this! I'll . . ."

Jessica reached into her dress pocket and brought her pistol up. She aimed and fired before Longarm could react. Her bullet wasn't meant to kill the attorney, only scare the man half to death . . . and it was effective as it shattered a picture on the man's wall.

Lee Monroe dropped his pants and tried to dive behind his desk. "Don't kill me! Please don't kill me!"

"Get up," Longarm ordered, his voice hard and flat.

"No, she'll shoot me!"

Longarm went around behind the desk and grabbed the half-naked attorney and hauled him erect. "You're going to write a statement saying that you have had nothing to do with any legal title to the Ray house on Plum Street and that . . . to your knowledge . . . Jessica Ray and her father have clear title to that property."

"All right!" he yelled. "Just don't let her kill me! The woman is insane!"

Longarm turned to Jessica. "You need to step outside while I finish up here with attorney Monroe."

"Gladly," she said, voice dripping with contempt.

Once they were alone, Longarm took a chair while the attorney wrote out a statement. When Longarm read it and was satisfied, he folded it up and placed it into his pocket. "How much did you make on the property?"

"What do you mean?"

"I mean how much did Willard Paxton and his brothers pay you to falsify ownership documents and let them have false title to the house?"

"I don't know what you're talking about! You got what you came for, now get out of my office."

Longarm walked around the desk that separated them and once more he backhanded the crooked attorney, this time sending him reeling across the room. Monroe covered his face with his hands. "Please," he whispered. "No more."

"I've watched you in the courtroom before. I've seen how you've twisted the truth and lied and intimidated people to your advantage. You're a disgrace to your profession, Monroe. Give me all the money you have here."

"What! You're robbing me!"

"No, you're going to pay Miss Ray for the mental anguish and trouble you've caused her with your dishonesty. Now, get the money."

"It's in my pants over on that chair."

Longarm found the man's wallet and emptied it. He counted the bills and saw that the cash added up to nearly two hundred dollars. "This will do," he said.

"I will have you thrown in jail and you'll never be set free if I have anything to do with it," Monroe said, voice trembling.

In reply, Longarm drove a wicked uppercut that shattered Lee Monroe's nose and dropped him sobbing to his expensive carpet. Then, without another word, Longarm left the office.

Outside, Jessica was talking to Cynthia, who was tossing some of her personal belongings into a box.

"I suppose," Longarm said, "I should apologize to both of you ladies for what you had to see in there. It was a pretty disgusting sight."

"You don't owe me an apology," Cynthia told him. "I've seen it all before. I . . . I had to do what that woman was doing to get the job when I was desperate without anywhere to go or anyone to turn to."

"What will become of you now?" Jessica asked as Cynthia finished cleaning out the desk.

"Believe it or not, I learned some legal skills in this office . . . enough to land me a job with another and this time ethical attorney. But right now, I need a little time to settle my thoughts and rid my mind of this filthiness."

"Until then," Jessica said, "I could sure use some help cleaning up my house on Plum Street."

Cynthia looked up and managed a smile. "Yes, it is such a nice place."

"You've seen it?" Jessica asked with surprise.

"Sure. Lee took me over there once and we spent a few hours on the bed, the table, and the floor. I'm sorry."

"Then maybe you won't mind helping me clean it all up," Jessica told the receptionist.

"I think that is the least I can do for you," Cynthia told her as they all overheard Lee Monroe sobbing loudly through his office door. She looked to Longarm. "Marshal Long, did you hurt him pretty bad?"

"I blackened his eyes, broke his nose, and maybe his right cheekbone," Longarm told her. "He's not going to want to go into a courtroom for quite a while."

"Good!"

Longarm smiled at the two attractive women and they all left the office feeling as if it had been a very productive although brief and violent meeting.

Chapter 9

Jessica showed up unexpectedly on Friday at the Federal Building and when she walked into Longarm's office, everyone stared. "Custis, could we talk for a few minutes?"

He came out of his desk chair to take her arm and lead her into a hallway. "What's going on?"

"That nice fella that you recommended has already found a buyer for my house," Jessica told him. "The people want to move in this weekend and Cynthia and I have it all cleaned up. I'd have liked to have it repainted, but the couple said they'd take care of that and they seem eager to move in because the wife is expecting a baby."

"That's good news," Longarm said. "Cynthia was a big help."

"I couldn't have done it without her. She's going to start looking for a job with another attorney and expects to have no trouble."

"I doubt that Monroe is going to give her much of a recommendation."

"Cynthia says all the other attorneys in Denver know he is an embarrassment to their profession so whatever dirt he may dish at her won't be harmful."

"Well," Longarm said, "that about does it, I guess."

"Does it?" Jessica asked. "I'll have the money from the sale on Monday and I plan to get on a train and head back to Arizona that same afternoon. My father is counting on me to come to his aid. But . . . but I'm not too sure that I can handle the claim jumpers and see everything through successfully."

Longarm knew what was coming and he'd already put a lot of thought into his answer.

"So," Jessica continued, "I was wondering if . . . if you could take some time off and come with me to Yuma."

Her eyes were pleading, and although Longarm knew the June temperatures in southern Arizona would already be scorching, he just didn't have the heart to refuse this brave young woman.

"I'd like you to meet my boss, Billy Vail."

Jessica blinked. "Why?"

"Because he knew your father and mother. Billy remembers what a credit your father was to our profession and to this federal office. I think, if you were to meet him and ask him if he would give me some time off to help you in Yuma, he'd be hard-pressed to refuse."

"Really?"

"Yeah."

Jessica lifted up on her toes and kissed Longarm, then slipped her arm through his and said, "Show me the way, Marshal Long."

Billy was poring over his reports and paperwork when Longarm knocked on his door and was bid entry. When Billy saw Jessica, he popped out of his chair like a puppet on a string. "Well, you must be Tom Ray's daughter, Jessica!"

"That's right. Nice to meet you."

"Sit down. You, too, Custis."

"Thanks," Custis said, barely able to conceal his amusement.

"Custis has told me a lot about you, Jessica."

"Hopefully not everything."

Billy blushed deeply. "Uh . . . uh, he said that you were here for only a short while and that he was able to help you reclaim your house on Plum Street."

"That's right. I couldn't have done it without his help. You have a wonderful deputy working for you, Mr. Vail."

"Well . . . well, sure. Custis is actually quite a legend. Sometimes, like this weekend at the Buffalo Saloon, he creates a lot of trouble . . . but he more than makes up for it in other ways. There is not a better man in the building."

"Thanks, Boss."

Billy offered him a smile before he returned his attention to Jessica. "Now, what is this I hear about your father being sentenced to life in the Yuma penitentiary?"

"Sadly, it's true."

"I knew your father and even though I'm sure he changed after your mother was killed in that horrible accident, he must still be a fine man."

"He is," Jessica agreed. "He defended himself in a Yuma saloon against two card cheats and when they drew their guns, he had no choice but to do the same. My father, as you may remember, was quite the shootist."

"Yes, he had the reputation for being both fast and accurate, and I'm sure he still is even though he's gotten a bit up in years."

"Father is only fifty-three," Jessica said a bit defensively. "But as you are aware, a lawman in a penitentiary is not going to survive all that many years. That's why I have to return to Yuma at once and now that I've sold my house here, I have some money to hire a good attorney to help clear his name and earn him his freedom."

"I understand."

"However," Jessica added, "I believe that the local authorities in Yuma are corrupt and that they have a part in this sad affair. I have no doubt that they are stealing our mining claim and reaping huge profits."

"But you've no proof."

"None at all," Jessica said quietly. "There were witnesses to the saloon shooting, but suddenly they turned mute. I think there were either bought off or scared off."

"I see."

"Good," Jessica said, "then you can also understand why just having the money to hire a good Yuma attorney isn't going to be enough to free my father and regain our profitable mining claim. What I need, Mr. Vail, is your best marshal, Custis Long."

Billy slumped back into his chair. "You're asking a great deal. I also need Custis."

"Couldn't you give me a time off without pay?" Longarm injected. "And I do have a few weeks of vacation time coming."

"Which I doubt you'd like to spend in Yuma during the hot season."

Longarm shrugged his broad shoulders. "You actually knew Tom Ray, I just mostly knew *of* him. Don't you think we owe him a chance? I can get to the bottom of whatever is going on in Yuma where neither Jessica or a local attorney could not. We both know I could be Tom Ray's only chance."

Billy scowled and studied his desktop for a moment before he looked up at Jessica. "What happened to your family was tragic. I know that your father deeply loved your mother. A loss like that could turn any man into a hate-filled, angry person. Can you really tell me that he shot those two men in the Yuma saloon in self-defense?"

"I can tell you that without a trace of doubt, Mr. Vail. My father was set up. I'm sure that the men who tried to cheat him didn't know who he was or what he was capable of doing with his gun. Most likely, they were just running their usual crooked poker game. But when they died, the marshal in Yuma saw his chance and I suspect that the judge there is part of this entire scheme to put my father into a prison where he will be murdered sooner or later. After my father is dead, the path will be cleared to sending thugs out to our mining claim so they can take it over."

Billy turned to Longarm. "It sounds like a hornet's nest of trouble to me. Are you willing to go to Yuma and try to set things right even if Tom Ray is guilty as charged?"

"I am," Longarm replied.

"In that case, I'll authorize your vacation time. I do know a captain stationed at Fort Yuma and although he won't be able to help you in a civilian dispute, he might know of someone who can. His name is Captain Maxwell Rodgers and I haven't heard from him in five or six years so it is very possible he has been reassigned or he might have retired just to get out of that awful desert country."

"If I need his advice, I'll visit the fort and see if he's still there," Longarm said, knowing that involving anyone in the army would probably cause him more trouble than it would be worth.

"Just as a resort. And if he is still at the fort, give him and his wife my regards."

"How did you know him?" Longarm asked.

"We were childhood friends and he wanted to be a soldier from a young age . . . though I doubt he wanted to be stationed in a place like Yuma."

"It isn't all bad," Jessica said defensively. "Our winters are wonderful and it is fun to fish and swim in the Colorado River."

"I'm sure," Billy Vail said without enthusiasm as he rose back to his feet and extended his hand. "Best of luck to you both! And Custis, you will keep me informed of any . . . troubles and reflect well on your office."

"As always, sir."

Billy rolled his eyes and went back to his papers.

"He seemed very nice," Jessica said as they were getting ready to leave the Federal Building. "And it's clear that he holds you in the highest regard."

"And that he also held your father in the highest regard," Longarm reminded the young woman. "That's the primary reason why he is allowing me to go with you."

"Well," Jessica said, "no matter what the reason, I'm very grateful."

"And I expect you will show me how grateful you are when we get back to my place."

She laughed. "Are you . . . you leveraging your help to get sexual favors, Custis?"

"I'm going to leverage something all right," he told her with a chuckle, "and I'm sure you know what!"

They both laughed then as they walked arm in arm down Colfax Avenue toward Longarm's living quarters knowing they had a long and enjoyable weekend ahead of them before they boarded a train bound for hell.

Chapter 10

Ten days later, Longarm and Jessica climbed off the Southern Pacific Railroad in Yuma, tired, hot, and somewhat out of sorts. On their way across southern Arizona, the conductor had been more than happy to give them a little local history concerning the riverfront town. Located at the junction of the Gila and Colorado rivers, Yuma had at first become an important crossing on the road from Sonora to California, and the Spanish had established an early mission on the California side of the river. But only a few years later, the local Indians had massacred everyone, and it wasn't until the California Gold Rush that the United States Army had founded a fort on the abandoned mission site to serve as protection for the overland travelers bound for the gold fields. For many years, steamboats and the Butterfield Overland Mail had been the only suppliers of the fort, and then the railroad had arrived in 1877, which greatly boosted the activity and population.

"When this railroad arrived, suddenly the town mushroomed," the conductor said. "Land was cheap and city lots cost almost nothing."

Longarm didn't offer the obvious fact that, given the harshness of the area, land was worthless except for what gold and silver might be found, although some enterprising people had used the sandy shores of Gila and Colorado rivers to grow hay and fresh vegetables.

"After the Civil War, the Union Army established a garrison here that provided military supplies and personnel to posts throughout Arizona and the New Mexico territories."

"The Apache were pretty hard on the people in this part of the country," Longarm added to Jessica. "They raided on both sides of the border and were almost impossible to catch and control.

"Does a Captain Maxwell Rodgers still command what remains of the fort?" Longarm asked.

"No, he shot himself in the head about two years ago. His wife and kids buried him and left for the East. Lots of soldiers here committed suicide because Fort Yuma was considered the worst fort in the West."

"I'm sorry to hear that."

"Did you know the captain or his family?" the conductor asked.

"I did not. But my boss knew and liked him."

"He was a fine man. Took to drinking pretty hard after his son drowned in the Colorado and he just never seemed to be able to come back."

"Tragic," Jessica said.

"Yes," the conductor agreed. "Most of Yuma either works for this railroad or the penitentiary. Some have businesses in town and a few have mines and little farms that can be irrigated from the river's waters. There are traders and the paddle wheelers still ply the Colorado regularly. They take goods all the way up to Las Vegas. If I didn't work on the railroad, I'd work on a paddlewheel steamer. Being on the water is the coolest place around most times of the year."

"I suppose so," Longarm said.

"The old army fort is pretty much abandoned now but the quartermaster depot is still operating. This is the hardest country I ever knew but it does have its own beauty and the winters are mighty nice. The local chamber of commerce sees its future in winter tourism. You know, folks with rheumatism and a little money can come out her in November and enjoy plenty of sunshine and warmth all through the snowy months back East. I do believe that Yuma is going to be around for a long, long time, but me and the missus, we're going to retire somewhere a mite cooler, maybe up around Prescott which has a pleasant climate year-round."

Longarm and Jessica found rooms at the Oasis Hotel, a fine, two-story stone structure in the middle of town. Because of her father and the complications that were going to be coming their way concerning the mining claim, they took separate but adjoining rooms.

"There's an inside door connecting them," the hotel clerk said with a wink. "You'll have your privacy, and we have a little café just off the lobby that I'm sure you'll find to your liking. Hotel guests get ten percent off the regular menu price."

"Nice to know that," Longarm said.

"Rooms 202 and 203. If you need anything or find something wanting, just come down and I'll gladly take care of it."

"We'll do that," Longarm promised, gathering their bags and following Jessica up the stairs.

Once inside their rooms, Jessica collapsed on her bed. "I'm exhausted from the trip," she told him. "I'd like to take a nap."

"Lock your door. I'm going to check out the town and see what I can find out about that marshal that pistol-whipped your father and the judge who sentenced him to life in prison."

"Are you going to let them know that you're a federal marshal from Denver?"

"Not until I have to."

"Be careful," Jessica warned. "Marshal Jeb Beeson is smart and tough. If he suspects you've come here with me to get my father out of the prison and reclaim our mine, he'll be all over you."

"I can handle it. And anyway, this is a pretty small town so I doubt it will take Beeson long to learn that we arrived together. He probably already has that information. Does he have a deputy or two?"

"Two," Jessica replied. "Both tough men and completely loyal to the marshal. Custis, what are we going to do now that we've gotten here?"

"I'm not real sure," Longarm confessed. "I'd say the first thing we do is find an honest lawyer and set about getting your mining claim back. You sold that house on Plum Street for how much?"

"Seventeen hundred dollars."

"Is there a bank in this town?"

"Yes."

"First thing in the morning you need to deposit most of that sale money. If someone broke into your room while we're eating or about the town and stole the money, we'd be in a fix."

"I'll keep it on my person until it is deposited," Jessica promised.

Longarm left his belongings in his room and headed outside. It was about four in the afternoon and the heat was oppressive. He began to perspire and thought he should have unburdened himself with his coat and vest, but he didn't feel like going immediately back to the hotel.

A few doors up the street he found the Cactus Saloon, and he stepped inside, thinking that he'd find the interior cool and inviting. A beer and he'd mingle with the customers and get some information on Yuma and the lawmen that ran it. The more he knew about those who had put Tom Ray in prison for the rest of his life, the better his chances for success.

"Can I help you?" the bartender asked, offering a friendly smile.

"Beer."

"I got some in a cool place," the bartender said with a smile. "You just arrive on the Southern Pacific?"

"That right."

"What's your business?"

"My own," Longarm deadpanned.

The bartender didn't seem to take any offense at Longarm's abrupt answer. He brought a beer and a clean mug and then surprised Longarm by pouring himself a glass. Raising it, the bartender smiled and said, "Welcome to hell, stranger!"

Despite the desert heat and the desperate situation he and Jessica face, Longarm had no choice but to swallow the beer and smile.

Longarm sipped his beer and when he was joined by a

couple of workmen, he struck up a conversation. "You men live here in Yuma?" he asked.

"Sure do. Both of us work for the railroad on its construction crew."

"It must be kind of tough in mid-summer."

The taller and older of the pair nodded. "It's already getting into the nineties and we ain't even gotten into July and August. We start work at the break of dawn and don't stop until we quit at two o'clock. After that, it's too damned hot to do much out in the sun."

"You can say that again," the younger of the pair added. "But the Southern Pacific pays higher wages down in this part of the country in order to keep its crews up to size and speed. If they didn't pay extra, no one would be willing to stand it."

"That's true," the older man agreed. "Used to be the biggest problem was the Apache. Geronimo and Cochise, they were bad ones, and there were a lot of others that raided and burned folks out."

Longarm nodded. "I guess now there isn't much trouble around here, huh?"

"Oh, there's enough," the younger man said, draining his beer and signaling the bartender for more. "After payday, this town can get pretty wild. Lots of fights and sometimes a killing. Keeps Marshal Beeson and his two deputies hopping."

"I'd imagine so," Longarm said. "I used to know a man that got into a gunfight. Maybe in this very saloon."

"What was his name?"

"Tom Ray."

The two workers exchanged glances and the older one said, "Tom was a good fella. He killed two cardsharps right back there near that wall. Marshal Beeson and one of his deputies came rushing in and hit him from behind. Now, Old Tom Ray is serving life in the penitentiary."

"Ain't many that last more than five or six years," the younger man said. "They put them in these little rock cells with flat-iron straps in front. Those prisoners must bake in the daytime and it doesn't cool down all that much at night."

"Do they ever get off that hill?" Longarm asked.

"Sure they do. About once a week they force march five or six at a time under armed guard down to the river and let 'em soak and swim. They give 'em bars of soap and let 'em wash themselves and their own clothes. By the time they are marched back to their cells, their clothes are dry."

"I've heard that those weekly outings to the river are all that keep some of those prisoners from killing themselves. Why, they go into the Colorado even in the middle of winter when the water is damn cold."

"That's right," the other agreed. "And they got some women serving sentences there, too. Five or six, I hear. A couple of 'em are in for murder, like poor old Tom Ray."

"Are the prisoners allowed any visitors?" Longarm asked.

"Sure thing," the younger man said. "Every Sunday afternoon is visiting hours but you won't see any visitors come once the heat of summer sets in on Yuma as it is doing right now."

"True enough," the older man said. "Who would come all the way to this hell on earth to see a prisoner for a couple of hours when the sun can bake their brains."

"I see what you mean," Longarm said, draining his beer.

"Old Tom Ray has a pretty daughter and the word is that she just arrived in town on the train," the younger man mentioned. "I'd sure like to get to know her better."

"I'll bet you would," the older man said. "She's pretty. It's a sad thing when she has a father sentenced for life."

"I heard," Longarm said, "that they own a mining claim just up the river. One that produces gold."

"The daughter must have sold it because it's being worked by some men. I don't know who they are, but they come in now and then to drink, whore, and buy supplies."

Longarm figured he'd heard about as much as he was going to get from these two men so he told them good-bye and stepped outside into fading light. It was still hot, but with the sun gone down it was cooling a bit.

Longarm lit a cigar and took a chair by the sidewalk, hoping that someone would come along looking for conversation. He didn't have to wait but a few minutes when a big man with a drooping handlebar mustache and two upper front gold teeth stopped to talk.

"Evening," the man said.

"Evening," Longarm replied.

The man took an empty chair beside Longarm and rolled a cigarette in silence before he asked, "You been in Yuma long?"

"Nope."

"You arrive earlier on the train?"

"That's right."

"I heard that you came in with Tom Ray's daughter, Miss Jessica, and that you took adjoining rooms at the Oasis Hotel."

Longarm blew a ring of smoke out toward the street, then he turned and looked at the stranger. "You seem to be a real observant sort of fella."

"It's my job."

"Then you must be Marshal Jeb Beeson."

The man inhaled deeply and let the smoke drain through

his nostrils. "I *know* who I am, but the question is . . . who the hell are you and what are you doing with the Ray girl?"

"What if I told you we were planning to get married and she wanted me to meet her father up on the hill this coming Sunday afternoon?"

The marshal was silent for a moment. "Well, I'd say that was a good and reasonable thing to do. However, if you were to stay in my town, then I'd probably come to believe that you weren't being completely honest about why you came to Yuma."

"I guess what you'll have to do is to wait until next Monday to find out if Miss Ray and I are on the outbound train."

"But you see, mister, I'm a very curious man and also an impatient one. So I don't intend to wait until next Monday if you're intending to stay here."

Longarm came to his feet. "Last I heard, Marshal Beeson, this was a free country where a man can come and go as he damn well pleases. So if you'll excuse me, I'm going to say good night."

The marshal came to his feet. He was almost as tall as Longarm and probably twenty pounds heavier. "What is your name?"

"Custis. Custis Long."

"Well, Mr. Custis Long, Yuma is no place to get married or have your honeymoon. If you have any sense at all, you had better be headed out of town with Miss Ray come Monday or I'm going to have all kinds of unpleasant questions for you to answer."

"I understand," Longarm told the man as he walked away.

"Long! You don't want to cross me!"

"No, sir," Longarm called back over his shoulder. "Wouldn't dream of doin' such a foolish thing as that."

"Glad to hear it, and congratulations on catching such a pretty woman even though she sure ain't goin' to be no virgin bride."

That last comment stopped Longarm dead in his tracks. He took a deep breath, turned, and walked back to stand toe-to-toe with the town marshal. "Marshal Beeson, you are not a gentleman and I don't like you very much."

Beeson laughed and blew smoke in Longarm's face. "Mister, you are a big man and you look tough. But I'm the most bad-assed fella you ever came across and my two deputies aren't choir boys. So if you value your health and you really intend to marry that girl, I'd suggest you be on the train come Monday morning."

Longarm withdrew the cigar from his mouth and studied it for a moment, then he smiled, shoved the cigar back into his mouth and walked away. He was just itching to jam that cigar down the marshal's throat, burning end first. Yet, the marshal had given him three full days to investigate and gain some answers before Monday. And considering that as a gift, Longarm decided to let the mean-spirited and uncalled-for remark about Jessica not being a virgin bride pass.

Chapter 11

Longarm sat across the table from Jessica and watched her finish her breakfast. "What are you up to today?"

"I'm going to open a bank account and put my house sale money where it's safe."

"Good idea."

"Then I'm going to go see an attorney named Kent Hamilton and see if he wants to take on the establishment here in Yuma and try to get my father's sentence overturned."

"You want me to go along with you?"

"No," Jessica said. "Kent is honest and he's always been very smitten with me. I think he'd do a good job for my father."

"He may not even want to get involved," Longarm said. "Yuma is a small town run by a corrupt marshal and we've already considered that the judge himself may be in cahoots with Marshal Beeson."

"All I can do is ask him to help and offer to pay him well. When I left here to go to Denver I had forty-seven dollars and not much hope. But now I return with you and the sale money from the Denver house. So the way I see things, Custis, is that I'm doing a whole lot better than I was before."

"That's a good way to look at it."

"What about you?"

Longarm frowned. "I think I'm going to rent a horse and ride up to your mining claim."

"I should go with you," Jessica said.

"No, I'd rather go alone so they don't know who I am."

"They might shoot on sight."

"I doubt that, but I'll just have to take my chances."

Jessica nodded. "All right. I guess we'll meet back up in our hotel rooms later today."

"That's the plan," Longarm told her.

Jessica and Longarm finished their breakfast and went their separate ways. Jessica was eager to see Kent. A year earlier they had enjoyed a brief, but steamy romance and she knew that Kent still carried a strong torch for her. So when she entered his office it was no surprise to see the delight on his handsome face.

"Why, Jessica! How good it is to see you again!" he said, hurrying forward to give her a powerful embrace and then a kiss. "You've been on my mind since the last time we saw each other and I've been visiting your father up on Prison Hill every Sunday."

"How is he doing?"

Kent's smile faded. "I hate to tell you this but he's aging fast and has lost quite a bit of weight. I take him extra food that I get at the bakery and he enjoys it, but . . ."

"Thank you for doing that."

"You know he and I have always been good friends. He thought we were going to be married."

"Maybe, if things had gone just a little differently, I would have married you."

"I proposed and my offer still stands," Kent said. "We made quite the couple here in Yuma."

"We did," she agreed, pulling away from his arms. "I sold my house in Denver and I've come back to hire you to help my father."

"I'd have helped him without expecting payment."

"I know. But I want to pay you anyway. How much do you want?"

"I can use some payment," he admitted. "I work alone but this office isn't cheap to rent and I have parents in New Mexico that I send money to every month the same as my oldest brother does. Without our help, they'd be in a bad situation as my father is in poor health and needs a lot of medical attention."

"You're a good son," Jessica said. "And I feel better paying you for your services."

He turned and walked over to his desk. "If I really go to work trying to free your father, my life is going to be in danger. I may have to leave Yuma before this is over in order to stay alive."

"I understand that."

"Then understand this," Kent said. "I want a dollar an hour and I want us to be like we were before."

Jessica thought about what she should say or do next. Kent Hamilton was her father's only hope and he was desperately in love with her and had been for years. He wanted to marry her. So what else could she do but go along with his demands?

"All right," she said quietly as she reached up and began to unbutton her blouse. "Let's seal this agreement."

He gaped. "Do you mean right here and now?"

She went over and locked his door then pulled the shade down over his front window. "That's *exactly* what I mean."

Suddenly, his eyes were glazed with passion and he watched as she removed her clothing, slowly, seductively. He licked his lips and began to undress.

"Oh, gawd, Jessie," he panted. "You have no idea of how often I've fantasized that this was going to happen."

"I'm willing to do whatever it takes to get my father free and our mine back," she said honestly. "But I don't want you killed."

"Do you . . . do you love me?" he asked, desperation in his voice as he came and took her into his arms.

"I . . . I might," she confessed. "I don't know. With my father in prison and with all the terrible things that have happened . . . my mind is confused."

Kent reached down and his finger found its way between her silken thighs. He kissed her lips until she felt as if she was going to swoon and then he knelt before her and his tongue slipped into her wetness. Jessica moaned and spread her legs, backing up against the wall as he pushed and probed.

"Kent," she breathed, knowing she should have told him about Longarm but afraid that he would have been so hurt that he'd have refused to help. "Oh, Kent!"

His tongue and fingers knew exactly what she liked best and when her legs began to tremble and she felt she was about to collapse, he led her to his big leather couch and laid her down saying, "Just like old times, Jessie. Just like it used to be with us."

Jessica felt his rod enter her and she found she was eager to take all of him in a rush. Her long legs wrapped themselves around his narrow waist and she groaned with pleasure as he began to thrust.

"Just like old times," she breathed. "You were my very first and it was on this same couch."

"Yeah," he panted, thrusting hard and grinning hugely. "I never forgot and I'm glad you didn't, either. You were my only virgin, Jessie, and I never had another woman on this couch . . . none would have compared."

"But you have had other women."

"Oh, yeah," he grunted, slamming his rod in and out of her slick honey pot. "But you've always been the only one that I've loved. Ever will love. Come on, Jessie, come on and let go!"

And then Jessica *did* let go. Her entire body began to shake and her fingernails scratched his back as her body convulsed, and she cried out, feeling a hot rush explode between her legs. He took her so violently and with such passion that she knew that he had not released his seed in a long time. Kent just kept giving it to her until she felt limp and began to laugh for no reason at all.

Kent took her once more, this time as she leaned over his desk and he came into her from behind. She had always loved to have him take her that way and his rod touched places that had not been touched even by Longarm, who was even more skillful as a lover but who did not love her.

When Kent cried out and slammed himself up into her while roaring his delight, Jessica laid her head down on his desk and smiled knowing that he would do anything to help her get her father out of prison and when he did, she would marry him just as her father had always hoped.

"Kent," she said a short while later, still naked as they sat on his leather couch holding hands.

"Yeah."

"I came back with a man."

"Is he your lover . . . or . . ."

"We've made love."

"Is he in love with you?"

"No. He's definitely not."

Kent looked into her eyes. "Are you . . ."

"No," she said. "I'm not in love with him, either."

"Then why did he come back with you?"

"It's a long story."

"I want to hear it all."

And so Jessie told him and when she was finished, he said, "I can't even think about you being in adjoining hotel rooms and making love with him while we do the same."

"I'll get another room."

"Not good enough," Kent Hamilton said, his voice firm and final. "We're going to find a justice of the peace and be married today. You'll become my wife before he returns to Yuma."

"Or you won't help my father?" she asked. "Even after what we've just done and what we mean to each other?"

"Yes, even after all that." Kent began to dress. "If I thought you were in love with him or making love with him . . . it would destroy me after what we've just done here. Marry and move in with me . . . or I'm sorry but we're done. My heart just won't stand up to more pain or loss."

She understood and began to gather her clothes. She needed a towel to soak up his seed, which was running down the insides of her legs. "Kent, I'm a mess. Please find me a towel or something and then we'll get dressed and get married."

"What is the marshal going to do when he finds out you're no longer willing to go to his bed?"

"I don't know."

"Will he just get back on the train and leave for Denver?"

"I don't think so. Part of the reason he's doing this is that he knows how much my father meant to his department and boss in Denver."

"And the other part?" Kent asked.

"He loves to lay me down just as much as you do."

"Well, if he leaves, we'll just have to find a way to help your father get out of prison without his help."

"I guess so," Jessica said. "But when you meet Marshal Custis Long, you'll understand why we really need his help and protection. He's tough and determined, Kent. He can shield us from Marshal Beeson and all the corruption of the man's office."

Kent nodded with understanding. "Okay, but he has to realize that once we're married, he'll no longer get to bed you."

"He'll understand. At heart, he's a southern gentleman. And besides, Custis is the kind of man who can find women quickly and easily. He won't be heartbroken and he won't be jealous or resentful."

"Given how you look and make love I find that pretty hard to believe."

"Believe it," she told him. "Custis Long isn't a man whose heart can ever be broken by a woman . . . any woman . . . even me."

Kent came over and kissed her breasts before she could finish covering herself. "After we're married we can't go away and have a proper honeymoon."

"No," she said, realizing that was true.

"But we will, Jessie. When we've gotten your father free and all this bad stuff is past, we're going somewhere beautiful and we'll have that honeymoon that we used to talk about."

"You talked about."

"All right, so I talked about it all the time. But it's going to come true," Kent vowed. "With you as my wife, I can't be stopped by anyone or anything."

Jessica pulled his face into the soft mounds of her breasts. "Kent," she whispered, "I don't deserve you."

"Probably not," he agreed. "But then who said people get what they deserve . . . for good or for ill . . . in this world?"

Jessie hugged him tightly. She was going to be married within the hour and she had no earthly idea what Longarm would do or say when he found out.

Chapter 12

Longarm had bought four bottles of the saloon's cheapest whiskey and then he'd rented a skinny, bigheaded blue roan. However, it had an easy gait and wasn't lazy so he had no complaints. As he splashed across the Gila River, riding north, he was thinking about how he would react if he were fired upon by the claim jumpers. No doubt he should have brought his Winchester instead of just a sidearm, but he hadn't wanted to provoke a fight when he would be badly outnumbered. His hope was that he could ride onto the claim and pretend that he was making a little money delivering and selling whiskey. Maybe he would be invited into the mining camp and the claim jumpers would get drunk and talkative.

"There they are," Longarm said out loud to himself after he'd ridden only a mile or two. He reined in the gelding when he saw a sign hanging on a piece of mesquite with the crudely written words NO TRESPASSING! Longarm dismounted and tied the blue roan to a bush, then moved off

the road toward a low and rocky hillside that overlooked the
river. Flattening out on the hilltop, he studied the work going
on about a quarter mile north. Right away he saw two shirtless men busting rock, talking and laughing while another
pair came and went delivering wheelbarrows of ore extracted
from the mine.

Longarm studied the men carefully saw that none of the
men were packing pistols so he returned to his horse,
checked his gun, and remounted. Then, forcing a smile to
his face, he rode up the track, ignoring the sign, and came
right up on the miners, who were so busy at their labors that
they didn't notice him.

"Good morning!" he called. "You boys sure are hard at
work!"

The pair that had been busting rocks jumped up as if they'd
been shot in the pants and lunged for the rifles. Longarm
didn't make any attempt to go for his gun because none of
these men looked particularly dangerous. What they really
looked like were overworked and underfed prospectors.

"Hold up there!" Longarm called, raising his hands. "I
didn't mean any harm and was just following the river
north."

One of the miners raised his rifle and pointed it at Longarm. "Mister, didn't you see the sign that says no trespassing!"

"I saw a sign, but I never learned to read. I mean you no
harm."

"Turn that skinny blue horse of yours around and git!"

Longarm patted his bulging saddlebags. "Truth be told,
I'm a whiskey peddler."

All four men lowered their rifles and grinned. "You bring
some whiskey to sell to us?"

"That's right. Four bottles. You men look like you could use a little whiskey to make your lives easier."

"We could at that," a miner with a long, gray beard agreed. "We ain't been allowed to go into Yuma in more'n a week. When you work as hard as we do in this heat, a week is a long damn time."

"Sure is," Longarm agreed, trying to look sympathetic to their plight. "So I'll bet you boys have built up quite a thirst."

"We have," another man said, swallowing hard. "Nothin' sounds better to me than to sit in that Colorado River and drink whiskey while the water runs over my bare skin like the soft, cool hands of a woman."

"How much a bottle?" one of the miners asked.

"Two dollars."

"We ain't got eight dollars between us," another said. "But we got these rifles in our hands and you ain't got shit in yours. Maybe we'll just shoot you out of the saddle and take your whiskey, your horse, and any money you might be carrying along with that pistol you're packin'."

"You could do that," Longarm told the men, "but Marshal Beeson and his deputies consider me a friend and they'd be pretty unhappy about you robbing and then killing me."

"Marshal Beeson is one of the fellas that hired us!" a miner growled, raising his rifle and taking aim.

Longarm suddenly felt sweat begin to trickle out of his armpits. "Sure he did, along with the judge."

The men exchanged questioning glances. "Are you friends with Judge John Thompson, too?" one asked, cocking his head a little to one side as if a slightly different perspective might lend him some important insight.

"That's right. They all like their whiskey and I sell it to them cheap. But enough of this foolish talk of killing and robbing. I came here in peace to try and bring some small measure of comfort and a little joy to your lives. So why would you want to kill me and put yourselves at odds with the marshal and the judge? You don't need that kind of added grief."

"He's got a point there, boys," one of the miners said. "Why, I'll bet he'd take four dollars right now for them four bottles and we could pay him the rest next time the marshal sends a couple of replacements out here like he promised so we can go into town and get drunk."

The smallest of the miners scrubbed his scraggly whiskers and nodded. "Mister," he said, still clutching his rifle. "You reckon you'd sell us four bottles and trust us for the rest of your money come our payday?"

Longarm sighed and made a big deal of considering the request. After a few moments, he said, "Well, boys, I can see that you ain't getting rich out here working in this gawd-awful country. When do you get paid next?"

"Next Wednesday. Surely you can wait that long."

"Maybe I can at that," Longarm slowly decided as he dismounted and began to open his saddlebags and pass the bottles around. "As long as you fellas give me your word that you'll pay me the other four dollars next week."

"Hell yes, we will!" the biggest of them shouted. "Won't we, boys!"

The other three nodded their heads vigorously and then scooped up the bottles, popped their corks, and drank fast.

Longarm loosened the cinch on his roan and tied it to a rusty piece of mining equipment. He glanced at the cave and then strolled over to the ore pile and studied it, looking for flakes or gold nuggets. The ore was heavy with pink and pearl-colored quartz and shiny. Longarm didn't know much about prospecting, but he did know that gold was often found alongside quartz.

The four miners were drinking fast and two of them shucked off their clothes and waded out into the Colorado River where they sat in the mud with the cool water running up to their necks and drank their whiskey.

"Give 'em an hour," Longarm said to himself. "Or maybe even less and they'll tell me everything they know."

The hour passed pleasantly enough. Longarm had to smile as the miners whooped and hollered and splashed each other laughing uproariously. But by and by they finished their bottles of watered-down whiskey and laid down on the muddy bank in a half-drunken stupor.

Longarm walked over to them and sat down on the bank far enough from the water where the sand was dry. All bare-chested and dripping wet, the miners were underfed, ribs clearly outlined. They had stringy muscles and oversized hands probably due to years of swinging a pick and clasping the heavy handles of wheelbarrows. Longarm knew that he had nothing in common with these men and he also knew that they weren't experienced with weapons. Most likely they had been ordered to keep strangers at a distance and work like hell.

"I hope you boys enjoyed my whiskey," Longarm said, matter-of-factly. "I can see that you don't have much fun around here."

"You can say that again!" one of them agreed with a lop-sided grin. "The boss comes around about every three days and he expects a couple of ounces of gold. We get paid on a percentage but I think he cheats us."

"Sure, he cheats us!" another said. "We ain't makin' all that much money considerin' how poor the food is that they haul out to keep us here. And we're expected to drink that muddy river water, too!"

"That's pretty hard," Longarm commiserated. "Your boss's name would be . . . ah . . ."

"Mitch Lang," one of the miners said. "He's the one we answer to but we all know he takes his orders from Marshal Beeson and Judge Thompson."

"Yeah," Longarm said. "I knew that. But didn't this claim used to belong to a lawman from Denver and his daughter?"

"That would be Tom Ray and that pretty gal named Jessica. Old Tom is gonna die on Prison Hill and his daughter ran off someplace. I expect they sold the claim before it started payin' out so good."

"Timing," Longarm mused aloud, "is everything in life."

"You can say that again," a miner said, nodding his head up and down. "My life ain't shit and I think it's because I was born in a damn thunderstorm up in the mountains and I was blue and my ma said I was colicky. If'n I'd been born on a sunny day like this, I'd have been a lot better off."

The other miners considered this statement with great care. Finally, one said, "Well, my ma said that I was born in a chicken pen in Arkansas and when she was birthin' me she got to thrashing around in there and I came out and slid across a bunch of fresh chicken shit! So my timing wasn't so damn good either!"

Longarm had to laugh, but not too much because the man clearly blamed his fate on the pen and the chicken shit.

"Oh," another said, "I was born well enough. My pa was

a coal miner in Pennsylvania and I was born dry, warm, and clean. But pa died in a mine cave-in and I had to go to work in the coal mines when I was twelve. So I started out in my life with good timin' and all, but it didn't mean much."

"What about you?" one of the miners asked, jerking a thumb toward Longarm. "You look big and strong. Is the whiskey business good to you and were you born with good timing?"

Longarm considered the question thoughtfully. "Tell you the truth, boys, I can't remember where I was born and so I don't know if my life started off good or bad."

"Humm," another mused. "It probably started off good because you look to be doing pretty well. And if you have a bad day, you can just get drunk on your own supply of whiskey any damn time you feel like it!"

"I could," Longarm said, "but if I drank all my whiskey up, then I wouldn't have any to sell."

"Yeah, I guess that's true enough."

Longarm had learned about all that he expected he could learn from these working men. The sun had moved over the yardarm and he was getting hungry and thirsty, so he figured it was time to ride back to Yuma.

"Say, mister," one of the miners said, wobbling over to stand beside Longarm. "It'd be doin' us a favor if you didn't tell Marshal Beeson, the judge, or anyone else that we took the day off to get drunk and have a few laughs. Think you can do that for us?"

"I sure can," Longarm promised. "I give you my word on it."

"We'll pay you that four dollars next time we're in town and after we get paid."

"I'll hold you to it." Longarm mounted the horse and waved to the naked miners sitting in the mud, grinning and laughing among themselves. He would return before long to reclaim this mine for Jessica and her father, and he sure hoped he didn't have to kill any of these poor, simple, and hardworking bastards.

Chapter 13

"How'd you like my blue roan?" the liveryman asked as Longarm dismounted and handed him the reins.

"He's a good horse and he moves well. I'll rent him again if I have the need, but I think you should feed him better. He's close to being skin and bones and is too good a horse to be starved."

The liveryman was a tall, heavyset man with a half-smoked cigar clenched between his yellow teeth. Longarm judged him to be in his late thirties.

"Well, mister," the liveryman said, lips turning down at the corners, "I wouldn't tell you how to peddle cheap whiskey and I don't much care to have you tell me that I don't feed my horses well enough."

"You look overfed," Longarm said. "So it just seems odd that you'd get to be hog fat and yet you half starve your ponies. Doesn't seem right."

The liveryman spat his cigar out and leaned in close on Longarm, who could smell the liquor on the man's foul breath. "Who the hell do you think you are comin' into town with that uppity young whore and . . ."

Longarm didn't wait to hear what the next words were to come out of the man's mouth. He slammed an uppercut into the liveryman's gut and when the man's eyes bugged with pain, Longarm drove a straight right cross into the side of his jaw and felt it break as the fat man landed heavily on his back. While the liveryman was down and howling in pain, just for good measure and because he'd called Jessica a whore, Longarm drove the toe of his boot up into the man's crotch turning a howl into a high-pitched scream.

"You ever refer to Miss Ray that way again and I'll kick your fat ass all the way up through your gullet!" Longarm hissed.

The liveryman couldn't answer due to his broken jaw and crushed testicles. He lay on the dirt floor of his barn writhing like a stomped snake in his terrible agony.

Longarm unsaddled the blue roan and led it into a stall and fed it a couple of pounds of grain; not enough to founder the poor beast . . . but enough to make it think that it had died and gone to horse heaven.

On his way out of the barn, Longarm glanced down at the liveryman, who was still curled up twisting and moaning. "You learn to mind your mouth or the next time someone might decide to shoot you dead. Hear me?"

Through clenched teeth, the fat man barely managed a nod.

Longarm made his way to the hotel and was about to start up the steps when the desk clerk called his name. "Sir!"

Longarm turned, one foot still on the staircase. "Yeah?"

"She's gone and I don't think she's coming back."

"*Who* is gone?"

"Miss Jessica Ray that you came in here with the other day."

Longarm was confused. He walked over to the desk and leaned on it saying, "Yuma is a small town so where did she go?"

"She went and got married."

Longarm was sure that he had not heard the man correctly. "Say that again?"

"She checked out late this morning and left this note for me to give you when you returned. I ain't read it, I swear that I ain't."

The note was written on hotel stationery. In her neat hand, Jessica had written:

Dear Custis,

I know that this is going to come as quite a shock but I married Kent Hamilton, the attorney. My father will be happy about that even though I knew you will not be at all happy. But I love, respect, and need Kent and he is crazy about me and is going to help get my father free. We'll still require your help . . . if you don't hate me. Please try and understand.

Sincerely,
Mrs. Jessica Hamilton.

Longarm carefully balled the note up in his fist and handed it back to the desk clerk. "Toss it in the trash."

"Sir, I'm sorry. I take it this comes as quite a shock to you."

"Yeah," Longarm managed to say. "It sure as hell does."

"If it helps, Kent Hamilton is a good man and he's loved Miss . . . I mean, Mrs. Hamilton for years."

"Glad to hear it," Longarm said, turning around and starting back out the door.

"Sir?"

"I need a drink," Longarm yelled over his shoulders. "Probably quite a few drinks. I'll be over at the Cactus Saloon if anyone comes looking for me."

"Yes, sir!"

Longarm *wasn't* heartbroken and he *wasn't* going to get drunk. Not with a man like Marshal Beeson looking for any weakness he could find in someone that posed a threat. But he would have a few drinks and buy a bottle of good whiskey for his room and then he would try to figure out what in the hell had happened between himself and Jessica.

Chapter 14

On Monday morning Longarm knocked on Kent Hamilton's door and fidgeted impatiently while he waited. Hamilton lived in a nice stone house with a small porch. In Denver, the house would have been considered extremely modest in size and appearance, but in Yuma it was one of the better homes.

The door opened and there stood the man that Jessica had married. Kent Hamilton was of average size and build, with a long sweep of brown hair brushed across his high forehead. He had good features and a wide smile with even teeth. He was clean shaven and dressed in a suit, white shirt, and tie as befitted a man of his profession.

"Good morning, Marshal Long."

The temperature was already in the low eighties and Longarm figured it would rise into the mid-nineties before the day was over. Longarm had not bothered to shave or have his clothes cleaned; he was irritable and aware that he cut a rather poor figure in comparison to the attorney.

"We need to have a talk," Longarm told the man. "Inside or out here on the porch, whichever you prefer."

"Come on inside where it's cooler. And I'm sure that Jessica would be hurt if she thought you were avoiding her."

"I'm not avoiding anyone," Longarm said too abruptly. "It's just that I don't like this town much and I'd never have come had it not been to help her and her father."

"And now that she has married me, has that all changed?"

"No," Longarm said with conviction because he had already given the anticipated question a great deal of thought. "I came to see if I could free a once very much respected federal marshal from prison . . . providing he was set up and killed those two gamblers in self-defense."

"Please come in where we can talk privately," Hamilton said, opening the door and stepping aside.

Longarm entered the small front parlor and smelled fresh coffee. Hamilton gestured toward a seat and then settled in close at hand. He called, "Jessica, Custis has come to visit."

Jessica appeared and damned if she didn't look happy and even radiant. Longarm swallowed hard and rose to his feet. "I guess my congratulations are in order."

"Thank you. Kent and I were together before and if everything hadn't gone bad so suddenly, we'd have married some time ago."

"I understand."

She moved close. "I do hope so, Custis. I wasn't using you."

"Yeah, you were," he said, trying to keep an edge of bitterness out of his voice. "But I came here because my boss knew and thought a great deal of your father. So now that our past is in the past, Jessica, sit down beside your new husband and let's talk about what I can or cannot do here."

"There is a great deal you can do," Kent Hamilton assured

him. "Starting with keeping me alive while I go through the evidence and petition a federal judge to come to Yuma and preside over a new trial with fresh evidence."

"Fresh evidence?"

"Yes. I have convinced a few witnesses to the shooting to testify where before they were too afraid to do so."

"Did you pay them?"

Hamilton shook his head. "They have some legal problems of their own and I've agreed to help them for free if they do the same for us."

Jessica smiled hopefully. "There were five men at the poker table when my father caught the pair cheating him and the others. Those other two card players are willing to testify that not only were the cardsharps working together in their crooked poker game, but that when my father challenged them, the pair of cheaters drew first."

"I see." Longarm frowned. "But unless we have a new judge, this fresh testimony won't matter."

"That's right," Hamilton quickly agreed. "We have to have a new judge. A federal judge coming in from the outside."

That made sense to Longarm. "But how can you possibly convince a federal judge to come to Yuma to rehear the case?"

"I can because he is my brother."

Longarm drew in a deep breath. "Wouldn't that sort of put you in a conflict of interest situation?"

"Normally, yes. But here are the facts. The two dead gamblers that Tom Ray gunned down had been in gunfights over cards before. They had killed a man in Taos, New Mexico, but got off clean. Also, I can prove that by putting Tom Ray forever behind bars, they were able to forge papers and take over his and Jessica's mining claim. I think we can get my brother over here and have the sentence reversed and all of this behind us in less than two weeks."

Longarm came to his feet. "So my job would be to protect you and Jessica until that happens?"

"That's right. And the pair that are willing to testify that Tom Ray acted entirely in self-defense."

"Who are these two guys?"

"They both work for Mitch Lang, who is tied in with the current judge as well as Marshal Beeson."

"What does Mitch Lang do here?"

"About everything," Hamilton said. "He owns the bank and the largest mercantile store. He has connections with the railroad and the paddle wheel steamboats so he actually controls most of the commerce that moves in and out of Yuma."

"And I expect that Judge Thompson, Marshal Beeson, his deputies, and most of the city officials jump when he snaps his fingers."

"That's right. Mitch Lang has a financial and commercial stranglehold on Yuma, but if we can prove that he was part of forging papers to take over Tom and Jessica's mining claim, I think we can break his power and maybe . . . maybe even see him and his cronies sent up to that prison on the hill where Jessica's innocent father now swelters and suffers."

"I'd like to see that," Longarm admitted.

"So would we."

"I'd like to get back to the two men who were at the card table when Jessica's father shot them. Who are these men and are they working here in Yuma?"

"No," Hamilton said, "they are working at the mining claim that you just visited."

"How interesting. Please describe them."

"Both are thin and missing several of their front teeth. Both are miners in their mid-twenties and sporting goatees and mustaches. They're nice fellas and . . ."

"I know exactly who they are," Longarm said. "I got them drunk and they stripped down and soaked themselves in the river."

"Their names are Albert Dodd and Carl Wittman."

"Do they know what we intend to do?"

The attorney shook his head. "They don't know anything other than what they told me they saw that night of the shooting. And I'll be honest with you, Marshal Long, if they think that they are going to be killed over this . . . they'll bolt and run like jackrabbits. The only reason they are willing to testify is because I can help them in a courtroom and will do it for free."

"And," Jessica added, "I've agreed to sell them a share of our claim for a reasonable price."

"Why would you do that?" Longarm asked.

Jessica looked to Hamilton, who cleared his throat and explained, "If we bring Mitch Lang, the judge, and the marshal down, my life and that of Jessica will always be in danger. Even from atop Prison Hill, deals are made and money changes hands. Lang has a lot of money and a lot of people that owe him favors. Sooner or later, he would kill Jessica and me so we've decided to move to Santa Fe when this is all past."

"There is a small item of immediate concern," Longarm said.

"And that would be?"

"Today is Monday and the marshal has ordered me to leave town on the train."

"You'll have to decide whether or not you are going to do

what he wants," Hamilton said. "And to be quite honest, Jessica and I will understand given all that's happened here if you board that train and never look back."

"Please excuse me for a moment. I need to think about this."

"Take your time," Jessica said. "And remember this . . . you owe me nothing. I . . . I am sorry about what happened and . . ."

"It's all right," Longarm said. He exited the house and stood on the porch while he thought hard and then he sat down in one of the chairs and studied the hot and dusty little street. There wasn't much moving around or going on this morning and he could see that this was a nice, quiet, and humble little neighborhood.

He'd never been run out of any town, not even one as sun-blasted and desolate as Yuma. And there were good, hardworking people living here under a corrupt judge and marshal and a man he had yet to meet named Mitch Lang.

But how could he guarantee the newlyweds that he could keep them alive until after Tom Ray was set free from the Yuma penitentiary? Or how could he guarantee that he could keep Albert Dodd or Carl Wittman alive, either, for that matter?

And what would happen when the train was ready to leave in a few hours and he was not there with his bags packed and the marshal and his deputies were standing in wait?

Well, Longarm thought, *today is likely to be even more interesting than yesterday . . . and that was saying something. So I think I'm just going to stay here and see this trouble through or else I'll always regret leaving a good lawman to die in a bad prison.*

Having made his decision, Longarm stepped back inside

and said, "I've never been run out of a town in my life and I don't see any point in letting it happen today. So let's play the hand out and see if we can get your brother to come over on a fast train and make sure that justice is served."

Jessica jumped to her feet and hugged his neck, crying with happiness. Longarm breathed in her familiar perfume and felt the soft mounds of her lovely breasts pushing hard against his chest. *Much better,* he thought, *if the lovely Mrs. Hamilton had rewarded him with a simple "thank you."*

Chapter 15

Longarm went back to the hotel, shaved, bathed, and had an excellent breakfast. He strolled into the hotel's clean and comfortable little lobby and bought a copy of the *Yuma Daily News* from the desk clerk, then he found a comfortable chair facing the front door and began to read the weekly paper. There wasn't much in the way of news, just some ads and two obituaries. Someone had ripe watermelons for sale and the local churches were advertising salvation. There was a marriage, the account of a man's dog being run over by a buggy, and a small fire that the town's volunteer fire department managed to squelch before it did major damage.

Two city councilmen were running for reelection, but they were facing no opposition, and the editor of the paper made a good argument that more of the town's citizens ought to get involved in politics. The school year was over and the teacher had resigned so the city fathers were looking to hire a fall replacement at the munificent sum of thirty dollars a month and a little house attached to the school building that needed serious repair.

"Good luck there," Longarm said to himself with a wry smile. He looked up, hearing the train blasting its steam whistle letting everyone except those that were stone deaf know that it was leaving.

He had just about finished the newspaper when his expected official arrivals barged through the door to confront him in the hotel. The marshal was flanked by two lean, tough-looking men, and they all looked as if they could bite through horseshoe nails.

"I thought I told you to be on that train this morning," Marshal Beeson said, legs wide apart and hands resting on his hips.

Longarm smiled over his newspaper. "Marshal, I got to reading this paper and thinking what a nice place this might be to buy a winter home."

"The hell you say!"

Longarm neatly folded his newspaper and came to his feet. His gun was loose in its holster and he was aware that he would probably die if he had to try to take out all three of these corrupt lawmen. Even so, he had to make a stand and he had to state his business honestly this time.

"Marshal," he said, "you do know that I came here from Denver with Miss Ray."

"Yeah, and I know that she married that gawdamn lawyer, Kent Hamilton, who has been a thorn in my side the last few years. That sure as hell means you have no more business in Yuma."

"Yeah, honest men like Mr. Hamilton usually do pose a problem for your type."

"What the hell is *that* supposed to mean!"

Longarm reached into his coat pocket and removed his federal marshal's badge. He held it up for all three of them to clearly see and said, "I've been sent here from Denver by my boss to investigate the killings that sent Tom Ray to prison."

"You can't be serious!" one of the deputies hissed.

Longarm stepped toward the deputy. "If I want to hear from you, I'll let you know. Until then, this business is none of your business. Same goes for you," he said to the other deputy.

"Now wait just a gawdamn minute here!" Beeson roared. "These men work for me and they take orders *only* from me!"

"Put a muzzle on them," Longarm growled. "Or I'll send them to the hospital and maybe the cemetery."

Longarm's statement, given that he was facing three armed and dangerous men, was so audacious that Jeb Beeson blinked and took a step backward. He paused and then seemed to gather himself. "So you're a gawdamn *federal* marshal, huh?"

"That's right. And if you give me any trouble, I'll send telegrams to Denver, Santa Fe, and San Diego, and you can bet your ass there will be other federal marshals coming this way before sundown."

The thin-faced deputy with the pale blue eyes whispered, "Let me take him, Jeb. I'll put two bullets in him before he clears leather."

"Try it," Longarm said, hand moving closer to the butt of his gun. "But if you're wrong, I'm not only going to kill you, but also the marshal and your friend with the tarnished tin badge."

For a moment, no one moved, not even seeming to breathe, and Jeb Beeson said quietly. "There is no need for a bloodbath here this morning so everyone just simmer down and relax."

"Now you're talking sense," Longarm said.

"What if I told you that the evidence against Tom Ray was overwhelming that he got a fair trial here in Yuma?"

"I'd say I didn't believe it."

"But a judge and jury did."

"A *paid* judge and jury."

Beeson's eyes narrowed. "That's pretty bold and dangerous talk. You got any proof to support your words?"

"Not yet," Longarm said with a confident smile, "but I expect to have some before much longer."

"Well," Beeson said, managing a smile of his own, "I think I'm going to let you stay a little while longer in my town just because watching you try to overturn a court decision is going to be amusing."

"Your amusement is likely to turn to amazement, Marshal."

"So you won't be sending out any telegrams begging for help?"

"If I do, you'll be the first to find out."

Jeb Beeson nodded, his eyes cold as those of a Gila monster. He turned on his heel and said, "Come along, boys. The federal marshal here needs to finish reading his newspaper and maybe burying his sorrows because he lost Jessica Ray to a third-rate, dead-broke attorney."

Longarm said nothing more as the three men marched back out the door. But off to one side, he heard a deep sigh of relief and looked over to see a desk clerk staring at him. "Did you find that interesting?"

"I never seen anyone face down Marshal Beeson and you did it with deputies at his side. For a few minutes there, I thought I was going to witness one of the greatest gunfights ever."

"You might see one yet," Longarm told the young desk clerk.

"Marshal Long?"

"Yeah?"

The clerk looked around to make certain they were alone. "I don't want you to repeat this, but Marshal Beeson and his deputies won't hesitate to shoot you down from the front . . . or the back."

"Thanks for the warning."

"I don't expect you need one given what was said. But I sure would hate to see you lose your life."

"What time is the hotel serving lunch?" he asked.

"Be ready in about two hours."

"Think I'll have a walk around town and come back then," Longarm told the kid. "Walking is healthful, you know."

"I wouldn't know about that, Marshal. But what I do know is that making enemies like those three isn't a bit healthful."

Longarm grinned and headed outside yelling back. "Tell your cook I'm going to be hungry."

"Yes, sir. And I wanted to say that I'm sorry Miss Ray married Mr. Hamilton. I expect you're taking it pretty hard. I know when my last girlfriend, Eunice, left me a few weeks ago I felt just awful."

"Her name was 'Eunice'?"

"Yeah, Miss Eunice Oxley."

Longarm shook his head. "With a name like that, I hope she was at least real pretty."

"She was pretty, sort of. But pretty big across the butt. She outweighed me by twenty pounds and had a mouth on her."

"So why did you feel bad about losing someone like that?" Longarm wanted to know.

"Well, Eunice was . . ." The clerk blushed.

"Go on," Longarm urged.

"She was a real bucker and sucker in bed. I never had a girl could do what Eunice Oxley could do . . . if you know what I mean."

"I know what you mean. Would you like a little advice about women?"

"Sure. You've had Miss Ray and she's the most beautiful woman I've ever laid eyes on. I expect you've had a lot of beautiful women in your life, Marshal."

"I've been very fortunate. But the thing is you ought to be looking for a woman who can be your best friend."

"What?"

"I'm serious," Longarm said. "You being real young still, all you're thinking about is how a girl can perform in bed. And I'm not saying that isn't important and that all of 'em are the same. Some will turn you upside down and inside out . . . and others screw like they're stirring stew in a pot and just want to get it over with. But if you can find one who is good in bed and wants to help you along in life and be your best friend and expects you to be *her* best friend, then you've really got something."

"I didn't know there were any like that."

"There are," Longarm said, "but they're not easy to find. Most of them are quiet, like deep water. They don't cuss and raise hell and jump into bed with anyone that strikes their fancy. They might be religious, but they might not. What's your name?"

"Montgomery, but everyone calls me Monty."

"Take my advice, Monty, look for the quiet ones and those that have sunny dispositions and a pretty smile."

"Yes, sir. Have you found that special one yet?"

"I have a time or two."

"Did you marry 'em?"

"Nope."

"Well, why not?"

"Sometimes things get in the way. Sometimes you let things get away. But I'm getting smarter every year. Not many women want to marry a federal marshal who is always going out of town. Most women want a steady man who comes home every night and when she lays her head down on her pillow, she wants to know that her man isn't likely to be killed on his job."

Monty nodded, concentrating on every word. "I never wanted to wear a badge."

"What do you want to do?"

Monty shrugged. "I'd like to own a hotel like this one."

"That takes a lot of money," Longarm told the kid.

"I know. I'm figuring on it. I believe that if a man works long enough and hard enough and puts his mind to one goal in life, he can hardly fail."

"I like the way you think," Longarm said, "and even though I'll never meet Eunice Oxley, I'm sure that you were fortunate that she left you for someone else."

"She did that all right. A gambler on this way to California. Eunice told me that he had proposed marriage and they were going to do it as soon as he made a pile of money at some high-stakes poker game."

"Sure," Longarm said, "and that will be when pigs fly across the Colorado River."

"Huh?"

"Never mind," Longarm said as headed out the door. "Monty, you'll do just fine in life . . . I'd bet on it."

Chapter 16

The day was growing very warm and just as Longarm was about to leave the hotel's dining room after a nice lunch, Kent and Jessica Hamilton walked over to his table.

"Hello there," Longarm said. "Care to join me?"

"We've already eaten and it appears you're finishing up," Kent said. "But we do have some news."

"Sit down and let's hear it."

Jessica looked excited and Longarm wondered if it was due to her recent marriage or something else. "Custis," she said, "my husband has convinced the warden to allow us to visit my father this afternoon. It will be a very private meeting between the four of us."

Longarm looked at Kent. "How did you manage to get the warden to make an exception to his visiting time rule?"

"Warden Thomas Gates is a good man and we know each other pretty well. I have sent some very bad men to his prison and we've gained a mutual respect for each other over the last few years. On top of that, he knows that my brother is a federal judge in Santa Fe, New Mexico, where Jessica intend to live after we leave Yuma."

"I see. Did you tell him that your brother was coming?"

"I did. Judge John Thompson will, of course, be outraged to learn that there will be a retrial and I expect he will file a formal complaint. But the facts are pretty clear and I've sent transcripts to Santa Fe on a regular basis arguing for a new trial. The warden knows that Jessica's father was unjustly sentenced and he is not friendly with Mitch Lang or Sheriff Beeson, both of whom he knows are corrupt."

"So when will your brother be leaving for Yuma?" Longarm asked.

"In two days."

"What are we going to do up on Prison Hill today?"

Jessica said, "My father really wants to meet you. He is extremely grateful and greatly encouraged by the fact that your boss has sent you all the way from Denver."

"Have you got time to tell me a little about the Yuma Territorial Prison?" Longarm asked. "I've never been inside the walls but I've heard that it is well managed."

"That's true," Kent said. "Warden Thomas Gates is a hard but fair man and he's tried to make the prison bearable for the inmates and the staff. For example, he bought a new dynamo generator so the prison did away with its gas lamps and candles. Now, the entire facility is powered by the generator and operates with electricity."

"That *is* impressive."

"The warden has also designated one cell to be a library. A call went out last year for anyone in Yuma who could spare a book or two to donate it to the prison library. And, there's a good medical dispensary as well as workshops for the inmates. They make all their own tables, cabinets, bunks, and chairs."

"He wants to keep them busy and occupied," Jessica added. "My father works in the carpentry shop, but there's also a blacksmith shop, a tailor shop, and a shoe repair shop. The inmates go to work very early in the hot season and quit around one o'clock when the heat becomes too intense for them to do productive work."

"Do many die of the heat?" Longarm asked.

"Very few," Jessica answered. "The cells are all dug or blasted out of stone so the walls are very thick and the interiors are bearable. My father says that the most common cause of death among his fellow inmates is consumption."

"What about escape?" Longarm wondered aloud. "Is that much of a problem?"

"No," Kent told him. "You saw the guard towers and fencing. And even if a prisoner did manage to get off the hill, where could they go? They are surrounded by desert and both the Gila and Colorado rivers have quicksand that would either trap or swallow a fugitive on the run. Add that to the fact that the Mohave and other Indian tribes hate most white men and would torture any escapees and you can see why almost no one tries to escape."

"Yeah," Longarm agreed, "I can at that."

Attorney Hamilton consulted his watch. "We can leave anytime. We'll have to hike up to the prison gate, but it's not that far."

"It will be difficult in this heat," Jessica warned. "But the warden doesn't like people bringing their horses up there and causing a distraction for the tower guards."

"All right then," Longarm said, paying his bill and coming to his feet. "How soon do we leave?"

"How about fifteen minutes?" Jessica asked.

"That's perfect," Longarm said. "I'll go up to my room and meet you two down in the lobby."

Longarm hurried upstairs, washed his hands, and changed his coat, then studied himself in the mirror for a moment before he locked his door and went down to meet Kent and Jessica.

An hour later and drenched in sweat, they were ushered into a small, windowless room. It had a table and four chairs but no pictures on the walls. Someone had placed a pitcher of water and four glasses on the table, which was very much appreciated.

"At least," Longarm observed, "it's still comfortable in here. Climbing Prison Hill wasn't the most fun I've had in a while."

A few minutes later, the door opened and a guard wearing a baton but no gun ushered Tom Ray into the tiny and Spartan meeting room. Jessica threw herself into her father's arms and hugged him tightly.

"Congratulations on your marriage," Tom Ray said to the couple. "I'm just sorry that I couldn't be there to give my lovely daughter's hand away to you, Kent."

"You were there in spirit, sir."

Tom Ray was thin, but still stood tall and very straight. His hair was silver and long, swept straight back from his high forehead. He had prominent cheekbones and pale blue eyes. Longarm could see little resemblance between the former United States marshal and his daughter, although it was clear that the father had once been a very handsome and imposing lawman.

"And you," Ray said, extending a work-calloused hand, "are Deputy Marshal Custis Long from Denver."

"That's right."

"I can't tell you how much I appreciate your coming to Yuma. Who sent you?"

"My boss, Marshal William Vail."

"Ah yes, Billy! I remember him well. I left office soon after he arrived and came to this part of Arizona with Jessica. I'm still not sure why I did that, but we scoured the local hills and valleys and after a lot of hardship eventually found a good claim and started to finally make some real money. But of course, once everyone knew we had found some gold, our real troubles began."

"I understand," Longarm said. "And I trust that your daughter told you that we were able to get your Denver house back not long ago."

"Yes, I heard all about that and I'm hoping that now that she's married the best attorney in Yuma, he'll see fit to forgo his usual fees for representation."

"Of course I will," Kent said, blushing. "Perhaps we should all sit down and have a quiet little talk. The warden was more than kind to allow this meeting but he did state that it should be brief."

"Then let's sit," Longarm told them, as he emptied the pitcher into the four glasses. "Cheers and to our good fortune getting justice served."

They raised their glasses of room-temperature water not commenting that the water itself was a murky and brown and that it had probably come right out of the river.

"So," Kent began, looking at the old lawman and now his father-in-law, "I told Custis a short while ago that my oldest brother, Judge Peter Hamilton, is leaving Santa Fe in two days and that I've filed all the paperwork to have a new trial over which he will preside."

"And you can do that?" Tom Ray asked with surprise.

Kent Hamilton colored. "I have to admit that I used some of that Denver house sale money to grease a few palms. Nothing new around these parts and the retrial will be open to the public."

"What about Judge Thompson?" Tom Ray asked. "He's not going to sit still for this."

"He doesn't have any choice. It's all been arranged and I'm sure that the courtroom will be packed as it was the first time."

"So what is going to be the big difference this time?" Tom Ray wanted to know.

"We are going to have some new witnesses to the shooting that took place. Witnesses that will claim you fired and killed the gamblers in self-defense and that they were cheating at cards."

"You found witnesses that will testify to that?" Ray asked, skepticism evident in his voice.

"Yes," the attorney said with confidence. "Mitch Lange and Marshal Beeson, as you know, took over your claim and two of the miners they hired were sitting at the poker table with you when the gunfight began."

"That would be Albert Dodd and Carl Wittman."

"Right."

Tom Ray shook his head. "He hired the pair to keep them out of circulation, and by giving them their jobs out at the claim he bought their loyalty."

"That's what he *thinks*," Kent Hamilton said. "But for a

modest price and a couple of one-way tickets to San Diego, they have secretly agreed to testify that you were innocent and acted only to protect your life. I've promised that they will go from our courtroom to the westbound train and then across the river never to be seen or heard from again."

Tom Ray nodded. "That's good because the moment that Mitch Lang and Marshal Beeson find out that that pair are going to change their stories and tell the truth, their lives won't be worth a plug nickel."

"You're right," Longarm said. "And so I'll have to protect them as well as your daughter and new son-in-law until after the new trial."

"Tall order, Marshal Long. Very tall indeed."

"There is no other way," Jessica told her father. "We either do this or you'll rot in this prison until you die."

Tom Ray smiled sadly. "My dear, I'm getting to be an old man. My life isn't worth the risk of you or Kent losing your lives. And the same goes for you, Marshal Long."

"We'll be the judge of that," Longarm said. "All you have to do is to take care of yourself here in prison."

Tom Ray's eyebrows lifted. "Do you think that they might try to have someone in here kill me before the trial?"

"I think that's a real possibility," Longarm said. "Do you have any current enemies inside these prison walls?"

"Not that I can think of," Ray said. "But you never know. If Lang or Beeson managed to get someone a little cash, they'd slit my throat without a moment's hesitation."

"Then guard yourself well," Longarm advised. "All this goes for nothing if you're murdered in this prison."

"I know how to protect myself and I'll be doubly on my guard now that I know what is going to happen."

"Good," Longarm said.

"The minute my brother arrives on the train, we'll also have to watch over him," the attorney told them.

Longarm frowned. "From what I'm hearing you all expect that this Mitch Lang will have his boys act right away."

"I'm sure that he will," Jessica said. "Mitch isn't about to let this new trial take place because it might expose his corruption."

Longarm considered all that he'd just learned. "Seems to me that I ought to meet Lang and have a little heart-to-heart talk with the man. Is he crazy enough to try and kill me outright?"

"No," the attorney said. "Mitch Lang is not the kind to risk his life in a gunfight. He'd rather hire others to do that sort of thing. But if he invited you to share a drink, you'd be wise to decline the invitation. Mitch is plenty capable of lacing your drink with poison."

"I see," Longarm said. "He's devious and a snake."

"That pretty well sums the man up," Tom Ray said. "Just be real careful. Marshal Beeson is dangerous, but you'll always see him coming at you. Having said that, he might order his deputies to ambush you from a rooftop."

"Custis," Jessica said, "until the trial that will exonerate my father is over, we are all going to be in real danger. I'm sorry to have dragged you into this."

"My choice to come and my choice to stay," Longarm told her.

A guard peeked into the door. "Need more water?"

"No, thanks," Jessica said quickly. "We are about finished up in here."

"I lock the door from the outside. Just knock and I'll let you out and return your father to his cell."

"Thank you."

Five minutes later, they were walking out of the prison yard and down the barren hill toward town. The temperature was well into the nineties and the sun was a burning hole in a pale blue sky. Longarm squinted up at it and then wiped his brow with his coat sleeve. *How, oh, how,* he wondered, *did anyone live here through the heat of summer?*

Chapter 17

Longarm walked into the Bank of Yuma, which was a single-story building made of limestone. It had polished hardwood floors and two teller cages in the front with several desks and a private office in the back. The teller was a man in his thirties who wore spectacles and looked pale and bookish. However, when he saw the sweat pouring off Longarm's face, the man said, "It's going to be a scorcher today."

"It already is. I can't imagine how hot it gets in July and August."

"It's not so bad," the teller assured him. "We get some rains that move up from the Gulf of Mexico and that helps cool things down a bit. Can I help you?"

"I'd like to see Mr. Lang."

"Do you have—?"

"No," Longarm interrupted as he removed his badge and showed it to the young man, "but I'm sure he'll want to see me."

"Please wait right here and I'll see if he's available. And your name?"

"Custis Long. Deputy United States Marshal Custis Long."

"I'll be right back."

Longarm didn't have to wait even a minute before the teller hurried out of the office and back to his cage. "Please step around that corner and follow me. Mr. Lang will see you at once."

"I thought he might," Longarm mused aloud.

He entered an office that was both spacious and richly appointed. Behind an oversized mahogany desk sat a man in his fifties with muttonchop whiskers. He wore an expensive gray suit and a gold-framed pince-nez perched on his hooked nose. The banker and businessman still looked strong and fierce. Lang came to his feet and extended his hand. "I have been expecting you, Marshal."

"I'm sure you have," Longarm said. "I imagine that Marshal Beeson gave you a full report."

Lang forced a brittle smile. "The marshal isn't too happy about you not leaving on the train. He thought you both had an agreement."

"Not at all," Longarm countered. "Beeson said he wanted me to leave and I said I'd damn well leave when I felt like it."

"You told Jeb Beeson that?"

"I sure did."

"Please sit down. Can I offer you a libation? Whiskey, perhaps?"

"No, thanks."

"I have some excellent scotch, if . . ."

"I didn't come here to have a drink with you, Mr. Lang. I came to tell you that Tom Ray is a former federal marshal and one with a distinguished record and many years of good service in Denver."

"Yes, of course I know that. But what Tom Ray did in

Colorado has no bearing whatsoever on his behavior in the Arizona Territory. Sadly, Tom Ray became obsessed with finding gold and becoming rich. I, on the other hand, always understood that becoming financially successful is the result of years of hard work and making prudent and sometimes very difficult decisions."

"Thanks for the insight." He waved his hand overhead. "Nice bank, and that's quite a big mercantile you own."

"I try to provide the people here with everything they need."

"I'm sure that you do," Longarm said, "especially those that do your bidding."

The banker smoothed his muttonchops. "You have a very direct and unfriendly manner about you, Marshal Long. But I am sure that I'm not the first to make this observation."

"I'm not in the business of making friends, and I know that you pretty much own this town."

"Oh, I wouldn't go nearly that far," Lang said modestly. "There a number of other very successful businessmen in Yuma, and more arrive each year seeking opportunity in the desert. But I'm sure you're not here to discuss the town's entrepreneurs."

"No, I'm not," Longarm said. "I thought I'd tell you that I'm staying until Tom Ray is released from the penitentiary."

"Ha!" Mitch Lang leaned back in his office chair and barked a sharp laugh. "Well, if that is true, then you are going to be here a very long while. In case you didn't know it, Tom Ray gunned down two men in the Cactus Saloon and was sentenced to life in prison."

"I hear that those two men were card cheats and that he drew his gun after they drew first. So where I come from, that is self-defense and not punishable by any judge or jury."

"You have your facts wrong," Lang insisted. "There was a trial, and the jurors as well as the judge ruled Tom Lang guilty of not one . . . but two murders. It is regrettable, but a reality. Tom Ray was actually quite popular, but you know how some men change when they've had too much to drink or are losing all their money at cards."

Longarm listened a few minutes longer while the banker talked and then he abruptly came to his feet. "I've heard a great deal about you, Mr. Lang. None of it is good. I'm here to inform you that I am going to see that Tom Ray is freed from prison and in the process it is very likely that the corruption that you and Marshal Beeson are engaged in will be exposed."

"You are sadly mistaken," Lang said, coming to his own feet with color rising in his cheeks. "And I would urge you very strongly to tell young Kent Hamilton that he is walking on thin ice. He has just married Miss Ray and now you and they should leave Yuma while . . . well, before it gets even hotter in these parts."

"For a minute there I thought you were going to threaten me."

"No threat," Lang said, managing a tight smile. "But this is a hard and unforgiving country and newcomers often make *fatal* mistakes."

Longarm had already decided not to tell this man that Kent Hamilton's oldest brother was going to be arriving in Yuma in a few days and would preside over a new trial. Why give the banker any more information or advantages than he already had?

"I guess we've about said all we needed to say to each other," Longarm told the man. "Oh, did your toadies tell you that Mr. Hamilton, his bride, and I visited Tom Ray this afternoon at the prison?"

The banker couldn't hide his surprise. "But it's not Sunday visiting day."

"That's true, but Warden Gates made an exception for us."

"I'll have to speak to the warden," Lang warned. "Rules are rules, and if he doesn't understand that, then—"

"If I were you," Longarm interrupted, "I'd stay out of the warden's business because you're soon going to have an awful lot of problems of your own."

"What on earth are you talking about!"

"Well, for one thing that mining claim just north on the river where you have men illegally working. The gold that you've extracted belongs to Tom Ray and his daughter."

"Not anymore it doesn't. I bought that claim and I have the papers to prove it."

"And I suppose they are locked up in your vault where they can't be examined by anyone other than yourself."

Lang folded his thick arms across his chest. "Marshal Beeson told me that you were an arrogant fool. You come into this town with Jessica Ray on your arm and you get adjoining rooms at the hotel. Then, Miss Ray throws you over like a piece of garbage, but you don't just leave Yuma a jilted and pathetic man. Instead, you mend your fences with the young woman and align yourself with a killer that is serving his time behind bars. Marshal Long, you need to return to Denver before you embarrass yourself or your office further."

"Thanks for the lecture and advice," Longarm told the man. "And I'm sure you'd like nothing more than for me to walk away and leave you to plunder that gold mine while its owner rots up on Prison Hill. But that just isn't about to happen."

"Marshal," Lang said, his voice trembling with anger, "I believe we have finished this conversation."

Longarm snorted with derision. "In truth, we're going to have a lot more to talk about before I'm done in Yuma. Good day."

Longarm left the bank without saying a word. But one thing he had learned from the visit was that Mitch Lang was going to stop at nothing in order to serve his own ruthless ambitions.

Chapter 18

Longarm was in his room preparing for a good night's sleep when he heard a pounding on his door. He picked up his pistol and yelled, "Who is it!"

"It's Kent! We were ambushed and Jessica was shot!"

Longarm threw open the door to see the attorney standing shirtless in the hallway with a bloodstained bandage on his upper arm. Longarm pulled the man inside and sat him in a chair. "Tell me exactly what happened."

"Jessica and I were standing on our front porch when two shots were fired from across the street. I heard Jessica scream and then I was knocked sideways by the impact of a bullet to my arm."

"Where is your wife now?"

"She's with a doctor and his wife over on Second Street."

"How bad is she?"

Tears were streaming from the young attorney's eyes and he choked with anger and frustration. "Jessica is fighting for her life. She took a slug in the side. I picked her up and carried her over to Doc Kelly's house, which was nearby. He got the bleeding stopped and the bullet out, but . . ."

Longarm had a bottle and he poured a generous amount of whiskey in a glass and handed it to the man, who was shaking violently. "Did you see who did it?"

"I couldn't clearly see their faces, but I'm almost sure it was Marshal Beeson's deputies. They took off running a few seconds after the ambush."

"Drink that whiskey while I get dressed and then I want you to take me to where the shots were fired," Longarm said, his expression grim.

Longarm dressed quickly. He had expected that he might be the target of an ambush, but he'd never thought that Lang and the marshal would be so low as to ambush the newlyweds. Still, it made perfectly good sense. With Kent and Jessica dead, it would be unlikely that Tom Ray would ever be freed from the Yuma Territorial Prison. And his brother, the federal judge, would probably be so overcome with grief that he'd be consumed with the details of a burial and then leave at once for New Mexico.

Twenty minutes later, Longarm and the attorney were holding up lanterns and studying the site where the ambushers had lain in wait until they had a good shot at the Hamilton house and its front porch.

"Just don't mess up the tracks," Longarm said, placing his lantern down on the ground and studying the footprints. "One man was wearing cowboy boots with pointed toes and the other was wearing round-toed shoes. Both men had small feet and you can see the cigarette butts scattered around."

"Anything else?" Kent asked.

"There are a lot of tracks here so I think the ambushers spent quite a bit of time in wait." Longarm studied the surroundings. They were standing in the front yard of a small, darkened house with a falling-down fence and high weeds in the yard. "Who lives here?"

"Nobody. The house is for sale and has been vacant for months."

Longarm picked up his lamp and moved up onto the porch where two rickety rocking chairs sat near the front door. He tried the door and found that the lock had been broken. Stepping into the house, he discovered more cigarette butts in a clay bowl half-filled with water.

"Kent, have you ever seen lights on in here at night?"

"No, but then Jessie and I didn't spend much time out on the porch. We were only there tonight for a few minutes admiring the full moon when the shots rang out. I thought Jessie was dead."

"Do you know what kind of shoes the deputies wear?"

"Never paid attention. But I do know they both roll their own cigarettes and you rarely see them without one in their mouths."

"Well," Longarm said, "we can say for sure that they spent more than one evening in this house, and when it got dark they snuck outside and waited for an opportunity to kill you and Jessica."

"And they almost succeeded."

"Yeah." Longarm left the house and went back to the site of the shooting. He studied the distance directly across the street.

"What are you thinking?" Kent asked.

"I'm thinking that they'd have killed you for sure if the light on your porch had been good or if it had been in daytime. But most likely they couldn't risk being seen over here in the daytime and so they just rushed their shots."

"What can you do about it?" the attorney asked.

"Not a damned thing."

"But if they smoke and you just said one has pointy-toed cowboy boots and the other round-toed shoes, then . . ."

Longarm placed his hand on Kent Hamilton's shoulder. "You're an attorney. You know that lots of men smoke and wear those kinds of shoes. Could you bring the deputies to trial with only that kind of flimsy evidence?"

"No, but . . ."

"I can't do anything just yet," Longarm said. "I think we should hurry over to the doctor's office and see how Jessica is holding up."

"Okay," Kent said, bitterness high in his voice. "But if I have to, I'll kill those murdering bastards all by myself!"

"Don't even try," Longarm warned. "In the first place they are professional gunmen and they'd kill you before you could get them both. And even if you were successful, you'd be arrested by Marshal Beeson and probably be hanged or at least sent up to Prison Hill. And then what good would you do for your new wife or your ailing parents in Santa Fe?"

"Nothing," Kent said quietly. "I'd be of no use to anyone."

"Exactly," Longarm replied. "So just let this pass for a while. I'll go see the marshal in the morning and I'll raise a stink, but of course he'll tell me that his two deputies had nothing to do with this ambush. Even so, I'll put them on notice that they're going to pay for this bloody act . . . one way or the other."

Kent Hamilton nodded. "Now I'm really worried. If they shot at us once they'll do it again."

"But we knew that from the start," Longarm said as they

headed for Second Street. I could tell the moment I met Mitch Lang, Marshal Beeson, and his two gunnies that this was going to be a fight to the finish."

The attorney nodded. "I'm sick with worry about my brother, too. He's on the train and he'll be here tomorrow. When he arrives and finds out that Jessie and I were ambushed on our front porch, I wouldn't blame him if he got back on the train for Santa Fe as fast as possible."

"That'll be his decision, Kent. But if your brother is a federal judge, he's likely been threatened plenty of times and maybe even attacked. I'm betting that if he's anything like you, he'll be all the more determined to bring justice not only to Tom Ray but to this whole town."

"I hope you're right."

Ten minutes later they were standing at Jessica's bedside in the back of the doctor's house. Jessica was sedated and sleeping. Dr. Kelly and his wife were cleaning up the room where they did surgery and when they were finished Longarm went to their sides. "How is she doing?"

"She's going to make it, but she'll be recovering for quite some time. The slug just missed her kidney and her spine. The young woman is very, very fortunate, but she's lost a great deal of blood."

"Did she say anything to you?" Longarm asked.

"You mean before I sedated her so that I could remove the bullet?"

"Yes."

The doctor looked to his wife who nodded. Coming to a decision, Dr. Kelly said, "Miss Hamilton told me that she saw the shooters who were hiding behind a broken-down picket fence directly across the street."

Longarm waited. "And?"

"She said she couldn't positively identify them but she was pretty sure it was the two deputies working for Marshal Jed Beeson."

"Thanks," Longarm said.

The doctor had a stern and craggy face. His eyes were sad and it was clear that he had seen a great deal of sorrow. "I understand that you are a federal marshal from Denver here to try and see that justice is served and that Tom Ray is freed from prison."

"You understand right."

"Then understand this," the doctor said, his voice shaking with anger, "our town is being held hostage by a few men who will stop at nothing to feather their pockets! Many of the best people in Yuma have just thrown up their hands and moved away because of Lang, Beeson, and his bully boys. Something has to be done and it has to be done soon."

"I understand," Longarm said quietly. "And I can only say this . . . things will change here and they will change dramatically before I board the eastbound train for Denver. A new trial is going to start in a few days for Tom Ray and he'll be freed."

"How can you possibly say that?" the doctor's wife asked anxiously. "The judge is a friend of Mr. Lang and in Marshal Beeson's front pocket. You'll never get him to reverse his judgment."

"He won't be presiding," Longarm said. "I guess Kent hasn't told you but his brother is a federal judge due to arrive tomorrow. And he will be conducting a new trial."

"Really?"

"Yes," Longarm said quietly. "And my job is to see that

he isn't murdered like Kent and his new wife almost were this evening."

"Marshal," the woman said peevishly, "I just hope you do a much better job than you did tonight!"

Longarm nodded, knowing that she was right.

Chapter 19

Longarm hadn't slept well that night, thinking about how Jessica and her new husband had been ambushed and nearly killed on their front porch. He awoke early and dressed with impatience, feeling a knot of fury building inside. The sun was just over the eastern horizon when he made his way downstairs and entered the hotel dining room. There was a waiter setting tables but it was obviously too early to expect to be served a meal.

"Can I help you?" the hotel waiter asked.

"I know you won't be serving for a while, but I sure could use a cup of fresh coffee."

"Of course! Sugar or cream?"

"Hot, black, and strong is my preference."

"Have a seat and I'll bring you out a fresh pot."

"Thank you very much."

Longarm drank his coffee in a brooding silence while the busy waiter finished setting all the tables and preparing for the first guests to enter the dining room. When Longarm had finished his second cup, he felt much more awake and less groggy. He consulted his pocket watch and saw that it was nearing seven o'clock.

"Thanks," Longarm said to the man after laying down a generous tip.

"Have a good day!" the waiter called as Longarm exited the dining room and then the hotel.

It was a bright morning and the temperature was pleasant and likely only in the high seventies. Longarm walked up and down the main street looking in shop windows. About twenty minutes passed before he saw Marshal Jeb Beeson's deputies enter the marshal's office. Longarm checked his gun and marched directly across the street. He didn't knock or give any warning at all but instead barged into the marshal's office catching both deputies off their guard.

"What the hell . . ."

Longarm launched himself across the room and drove a powerful uppercut into the man's gut, bending him double like a clothespin. The other deputy was wearing a gun, but Longarm scooped a paperweight off one of the desks and hurled it directly into the man's face, knocking him over backward. Before the deputy could recover, Longarm kicked him in the ribs hard enough to insure that there would be at least a few broken. Then he turned back to the first deputy, who was trying to straighten up and catch his wind.

"You sons o' bitches ambushed Mr. and Mrs. Hamilton last night," he growled as he grabbed the man's right arm and slammed it down on the edge of the desk. The sound of his shattering forearm was sickening. The man collapsed to his knees and Longarm booted him under the chin with the toe of his boot knocking him unconscious.

He turned back to the other deputy and kicked in the intact side of his rib cage. The man howled and began to sob.

"You are no good to anyone now," Longarm spat, fists balled at his sides. "My advice would be to get the hell out of Yuma before I decide to kill you both. What time does Beeson usually arrive?"

The one with the busted ribs was sobbing and writhing around on the floor, unable to speak. The other deputy was out cold.

"Guess I'll just wait for your boss," Longarm decided out loud.

He sat down behind a desk, sweeping it clear of papers so he could lay his gun on its scarred wooden surface. He consulted his pocket watch and saw that it was only a quarter past seven and figured he would have to wait several hours for Marshal Beeson to show up at his office.

Longarm came to the conclusion that he was too angry and upset to wait for the Yuma marshal and needed to seek the man out and have a confrontation. If Beeson decided to test him with guns or fists, Longarm was all for that challenge.

He stopped just inside the door and looked back at what he'd done to the pair of deputies. It had been quick and brutal work. He'd left both men too broken to fight or use their weapons for weeks, possibly months. That was exactly what he'd intended and needed to do. Now it was just him and the local marshal so the odds had been whittled down considerably. Oh, yes, and there was that viper that owned Yuma and controlled so many people . . . Mitch Lang.

"I meant what I said," he told the deputy who was barely conscious on the floor. "If I see you around here in a day or two, I'll shoot you on sight. Same goes for your pardner and you should tell him that when he comes around."

"You . . . you son of a bitch!" the deputy sobbed. "You'll get yours for this!"

A cold fury was on Longarm and he couldn't help but march back into the office, grab the man's gun hand, and then savagely snap several of the deputy's fingers. The man passed out.

Longarm surveyed his work and nodded with satisfaction. "One with a broken arm, the other with broken ribs and broken fingers. I guess that pretty much takes care of them."

He left the office and stopped the first man he met on the street. "Can you tell me where Marshal Beeson lives?"

"Sure, just over on Third Street. Yellow house on the corner. You a friend of his?"

"I wouldn't call it that by any stretch of the imagination," Longarm said, moving on.

Jeb Beeson was a bachelor whose wife had left him years ago after catching him in their bed with yet another whore. Jeb hadn't really cared. His wife had been a bitch and a whiner. Now, he was content to have a whore visit his house one or two nights a week to satisfy his needs. If she pleased him greatly, he would pay her . . . if not he would throw her out knowing that she had just two choices . . . keep her mouth shut about him and his savage ways, or get the hell beat out of her by one of his deputies.

Two weeks before he'd not been pleased by a woman named Loretta and he'd slapped her around and tossed her out of his house at two o'clock in the morning . . . naked, bleeding and yelling at the top of her lungs.

Somewhere, between his house and the whorehouse, a couple of men had caught and raped her in an alley and then they'd beat Loretta, almost killing her. She was discovered unconscious the next day and the rumors immediately began to circulate regarding Marshal Beeson's role in the savage attack and near murder of a woman. There had been immediate repercussions from a few of the outraged citizens including two ministers and Dr. Kelly.

"Pull something like that again," Lang had warned in his closed office, not hiding his fury, "and you'll be out of a job faster than a gawdamn snake's bite!"

Jeb Beeson had taken the banker's warning to heart. He had even paid Loretta's doctor bills and then bought her a one-way ticket to Tucson. In the future, he decided, he would not allow whores in his house but would go to their beds when his physical need was too great to ignore.

On the morning that Longarm knocked on Beeson's front door, the marshal was sound asleep. Longarm tried the door and found it unlocked, which was not surprising given the lawman's confidence in his intimidation of all foes.

Longarm followed the loud snoring into Beeson's bedroom and stood staring at the man for several moments, wavering between knocking him senseless in his sleep or prodding him into wakefulness and then laying down the new law in this town.

Longarm decided to do the latter.

"Wake up!" he roared, yanking the thin sheet that covered the slumbering lawman. "Rise and shine, you miserable bastard!"

Beeson was not one to wake up on the right side of his bed. He was a man that needed time to awaken along with several cups of coffee . . . especially after the previous evening's hard drinking.

"Huh?" Beeson groaned, trying to force his eyelids to become unglued. "What . . ."

Longarm had the element of surprise and he exploited it
fully. He grabbed the bare-assed marshal by the ankles and
dragged him off his bed. Beeson landed hard on his wooden
floor, head making a thunking sound much like when a
knowledgeable housewife raps her knuckles on a water-
melon to see if it is ripe.

Beeson tried to climb to his feet and Longarm watched,
almost feeling sorry for the man because he was fat and
flabby.

"I just paid a visit to your office," Longarm said, grabbing Beeson by the hair on his head and twisting hard. "And
I put your deputies out of business."

"What . . ." Beeson was coming awake fast. He tried to
grab Longarm and tear his grip from his hair, but that only
caused a sharp pain. "Ouch!"

"I'm going to tell you the same thing I told your deputies," Longarm hissed. "You need to clean out your office
and leave town."

"The hell you say!" the marshal roared. "Let go of me!"

Longarm shoved the man, glaring down at his pile of
soft, white flesh. "I'm going to either ruin you or kill you,"
Longarm said. "And quite honestly I'd prefer to do the latter. And although I haven't positive proof, I'm willing to bet
that you were the one that ordered your deputies to ambush
Kent and Jessica Hamilton and they failed. But I won't fail
to kill you. No, sir! So you've been warned."

Longarm didn't wait to hear the denial or the curses.
Instead, he turned on his heel and headed back to his hotel
because he was hungry now and ready for a good breakfast.
The gauntlet had been thrown down and all hell was going
to break loose today. If he was still standing when the train

rolled in from the east, a federal judge would be on it and soon there would be a new trial for poor old Tom Ray.

Yes, Longarm thought, reviewing the misery he'd just laid up the law in Yuma, *today is turning out to be damned interesting.*

Chapter 20

When the Santa Fe railroad train pulled into Yuma just before noon, there were not a lot of passengers that were unloading but the moment the tall, distinguished man with graying hair, mustache, and goatee emerged, it was clear that federal judge Peter Hamilton had arrived. He carried a valise in one hand and an expensive attaché in the other and his dark eyes seemed to take in everything at a glance.

Longarm had placed himself off to one side ready to intervene in case Marshal Beeson had recovered and found some replacements for his deputies. But Beeson was nowhere to be seen and now Longarm watched as Kent hurried over to embrace his oldest brother. After a few minutes, Kent pointed toward Longarm and the two men came to join him.

"Marshal Long," Peter Hamilton said, "we've never met but your reputation has spread far and wide. I can't tell you how much comfort it gives me to have you here helping and protecting us in this dangerous situation."

They shook hands and Longarm said, "Things here in

Yuma are explosive and it was brave of you to insert your-self into this situation."

Peter nodded and turned back to his brother. "Now, I want to meet your new wife and apologize to her for not being here for the wedding."

"Our wedding was a spur-of-the-moment occasion, Peter. We were married by a justice of the peace and surprised everyone in town."

"Especially me," Longarm added without a smile.

"Yes, especially you," Kent said looking a little shame-ful. "But anyway, let's go over to the doctor's office and see how Jessica is doing."

"Is there no hospital here?" Longarm asked.

"No," Kent replied. "Just two doctors and the infirmary up on Prison Hill. And besides, we agreed that Jessica was safer and in better care with the doctor and his wife."

"Yes," Longarm said, "we did. But she ought to be able to leave the doctor's office today or tomorrow and I think we ought to decide where we will all be staying until this trouble is past."

"We can all stay at my house," Kent offered. "It's small and . . ."

"Kent," Longarm said, "you told me yourself that your house was a furnace in the daytime. It's also too hard to protect against another ambush."

"So what are you suggesting?" Peter asked.

"I'm suggesting we stay in adjoining and upper rooms at the Oasis Hotel. There is only one stairway up from the lobby and a rickety iron fire escape that has mostly pulled free from its anchoring and couldn't support a child, much less an assassin."

"It will be expensive," Kent said. "But the hotel owner

does owe me for some work that I've done for him in the past. If several upstairs rooms are available, that might be the best and safest solution."

"I agree," Peter said. "And besides, we can overlook some formalities in this retrial but I think that if the presiding judge is not only the defense attorney's brother but is also staying in his house, that is pushing things a bit too far."

"Then it's settled," Longarm told the men. "Let's go see Jessica and find out how soon we can move her to the hotel. I know that the room that adjoins mine is empty."

When they arrived at the doctor's office, Jessica was sitting up drinking a glass of milk. Kent gave her a gentle kiss and hug, and then introduced his brother.

"Pleased to meet you, Jessica. I know my kid brother has been in love with you since way back when."

Jessica actually blushed. "I loved him, too, but as a friend." Her eyes settled on Longarm for the briefest of moments, and then she returned her attention to Peter. "How difficult will this retrial be?"

"Well, I'll need a day to file some papers and to study the court proceedings, but I think we can quickly select a new jury." Peter turned to Longarm, "Marshal, as long as we have those two witnesses who were actually at the card table when the shooting took place saying it was self-defense, then I can't see that the trial should take much time at all."

"I need to ride out with a wagon and collect them," Longarm said. "I'll do that this very afternoon and we'll also have to room them up at the hotel."

"More expenses," Kent said.

"I'll pay them with the house sale money," Jessica promised. "I can't think of a better use than to protect everyone.

Mitch Lang isn't going to just sit back and let us win. He's rich and he's connected to everyone in Yuma with money, power, and influence."

"She's right," Kent said in full agreement. "We'd be fooling ourselves if we thought that this was going to be a quick trial, full exoneration for Jessica's father, and then we'd all happily board a train for Santa Fe never to return."

"Denver for me," Longarm reminded them.

Dr. Kelly and his wife entered the room and were introduced to Peter. "I'm afraid that all of you need to step outside . . . except for the husband, of course . . . while we change Miss Hamilton's dressings and decide if it is in her best interest to leave this office."

"Believe me," Longarm said, "it is. Her life here is probably in even greater danger than before. If Mitch Lang and his cohorts can eliminate Jessica, then everything we're trying to do is bound to unravel."

"I agree," Kent said. "With my wife dead . . . with any of us dead . . . we all lose. Lang and Beeson will stop at nothing and you can bet that right now they are recruiting new guns and plotting their next move."

Federal judge Peter Hamilton nodded and stroked his long goatee for a moment. "I realize that I . . . having never met either Lang or Beeson . . . am the one least qualified to judge their future actions; however, it seems clear to me that their goal would be to prevent a retrial at all costs. And if they truly have unlimited resources here in Yuma, then we must constantly be on our guards."

"Are you armed?" Longarm asked the brothers.

They nodded.

"And can you shoot fast and straight?"

Kent said, "I'm a passable shot. Brother?"

"I'm probably better than passable," the judge from Santa Fe told them. "I've had my life threatened many, many times and I've taken it upon myself to become very familiar with firearms."

"That's good news," Longarm told them. "It gives me comfort."

"And don't forget that I can shoot straight, too," Jessica said with a hard look. "I wish that I had those two murdering deputies in my gun sights right now!"

"I don't think that you'll ever get that chance," Longarm told her. "I broke a lot of their bones just to make sure they were put out of play."

"So that means that Marshal Beeson will be looking for new gunmen," Kent said.

"It does," Longarm agreed. "But if we can get this trial under way and over with quickly, he won't have time to send out for the best talent."

"We'll need to move fast," Kent said, "because, if I'm reading this right, all our lives depend upon it."

"All right," Dr. Kelly said, returning. "I'm going to allow Miss Hamilton to move over to the hotel but she's going to need care and I'll stop by twice a day until this is all past us."

"Thanks, Doc," Kent said. "This way you or your wife won't be in any danger."

"That thought had occurred to me," the doctor admitted. He turned to Jessica. "You have had a very serious injury and once you are settled in at the hotel you need to stay in bed except to get up and be helped to the bathroom. Is that understood?"

"It is," Jessica replied.

"No going down the stairs, either. If you missed a step, lost your balance, and fell, you could start internally hemorrhaging and I most likely would not be able to save you."

"We'll carry her up the stairs and keep her comfortable," Kent promised.

"All right then, just be careful and I'll be over to check on you late this afternoon or early in the evening."

"Thanks, Doc."

They eased Jessica into a stout chair and then carried the chair up the street, into the hotel, and up the stairs. It was hard work and Jessica kept apologizing for the trouble she was causing. When they finally got her into bed, Longarm and Peter went downstairs and made arrangements for a third room. Then, Longarm turned to the Santa Fe judge and said, "I suppose you need to see the court records right away."

"Yes, I do."

"Then let's take care of that," Longarm told the man.

They marched over to the stone courthouse and when they entered and were shown to the records file, Judge Thompson barged into the records office. "What the hell do you think you're doing!"

"We're going to have a retrial," Longarm said. "Judge Thompson, this is federal judge Peter Hamilton. He's got the proper paperwork and we need to see the records of the trial you held for Tom Ray."

"How dare you come here and try to usurp my authority!" Thompson shouted. "I will not allow this. Get out of here right now!"

Peter Hamilton was very cool and collected. From the inside of his coat pocket he produced some official-looking papers and handed them to Thompson. "I'm sure after you've read these you will see that I have the authority to preside over a retrial given the new evidence that has surfaced and the fact that there are some obvious improprieties on your part, Judge."

"What new evidence! What 'improprieties'!" the man raged.

"It's all in those documents, and I suggest before you say anything more you read them very carefully. I also suspect that you might be placed on trial if we can prove that you had a hand in prejudicing this case."

Judge Thompson snatched the papers up and marched off into another office where he slammed a door. "Not too happy," Longarm said.

"If we can get some people to take to the witness stand and swear that Judge Thompson had a hand in seizing or fraudulently altering documents to obtain ownership of Tom Ray's mining claim and house in Denver then he very well might be going to the same prison where I'm sure he has sentenced many a man."

"Nothing would please me more than to see that happen," Longarm said.

A few minutes later they left the courthouse with several thick files regarding the Tom Ray murder trial.

"I'll go up to my room and burn some midnight oil going over these," the judge said in the lobby of the hotel. "What are you going to do now?"

"I think I'd better go out to the mining claim and collect our two critical witnesses," Longarm told the man. Their names are Albert Dodd and Carl Wittman."

"They're miners?"

"Yes, quite rough."

"Will they make creditable witnesses and be able to convince a new jury that Mr. Ray fired in self-defense?"

"I hope so. They need to be cleaned up. I'll get them rooms here and they need baths, shaves, and haircuts. Some new clothes and a little tutoring as to how to make their testimony."

"They do sound pretty rough," Peter said, looking worried.

"The last time I saw the pair they were drunk and naked in the Colorado River."

"Oh, gawd help us!"

Longarm patted the judge on the shoulder. "Don't worry. They're probably both illiterate but they're not stupid, and your brother has promised them a new life if they tell the truth about what they saw when they were at that card table with Tom Ray and the two dead card cheats. Once they do that with honesty and conviction, I'm sure that the jury will make it easy for you to declare Tom Ray innocent of murder because he acted purely in self-defense."

"Good. I'd like to meet them once you've brought them in."

"How about tomorrow after they bathe? I'm sure they smell to high heaven from working in the dirt and the heat. The Colorado River is cool, but it's muddy and I'm sure that they need some soap, a scrub brush, and a lot of buckets of hot, soapy water.

"Go get them straightaway."

"Consider it as good as done," Longarm promised.

Chapter 21

It was a very good thing, Longarm thought, that there were *two* liveries in Yuma because he was very sure that the man who had rented him the good blue roan gelding wouldn't be inclined to renew their relationship.

"Howdy," the man at the Rolling River Stables said sticking out a hand that closed around Longarm's like a bear's paw. "You're that new marshal from Denver!"

"That's right. How'd you know?"

"Yuma is not all that big and those two deputies you beat the hell out of bought one of my old buggies and left town just a while ago. My gawd but they were in terrible shape! I told 'em they should be in a hospital instead of heading out of town over potholed desert roads but they wouldn't wait."

"They were both rotten to the core."

"I know that," the liveryman said. "My name is Buck. Those deputies were a terror and people feared them. They tried to extort money from all the small businesses in Yuma and when they come around here they made it clear that they would start poisoning my rent horses, and if I *still* wasn't willing to pay, then they'd kill me!"

"So you paid?"

Buck threw up his big, work-roughened hands. "What else could I do? I have a wife and two fine sons. I didn't want to die and nobody would buy this business."

"Well," Longarm said, "you won't have to worry about that anymore."

"Maybe Marshal Beeson will hire a couple just like the pair that you beat almost to death."

"No, he won't," Longarm told the man. "And do you want to know why?"

"Sure!"

"Because before I leave Yuma your marshal is going to be either dead, run out of this town, or living up on Prison Hill."

Buck smiled widely. "That would be real fine! Now if you could also find a way to get sever the tentacles of that octopus Mitch Lang and send him packing, we might even have a future here in Yuma."

"I'm working on it," Longarm told the man. "What I need is a horse and buckboard."

"What for?"

"I'm going to collect some valuable cargo," Longarm said, purposely vague.

"I got a small buckboard and a good pulling horse that you'll like. But if you're heading up the river you have to be damned careful not to get my wagon mired down in any patches of quicksand."

"I'll be careful."

Buck looked into his barn. "How long will you be needing the horse and wagon in this afternoon heat?"

"If all goes as planned, I'll be back in three or four hours. Right about sundown."

"Good enough," Buck said. "You just set easy in the shade and I'll get you hitched up and ready to roll in no time at all."

"How much is this going to cost?"

Buck smiled. "It's free."

Longarm offered a mild protest. "Buck, you can't make a living renting out your horses and wagons for free."

"This time is free because I won't be paying any more extortion money to those deputies nor will my wife be worrying herself sick about them killing or beating me to death. Marshal, you're doing this town a huge favor and damned if I don't want to show my gratitude!" Buck pointed. "I see you're packin' a six-gun but no rifle."

"That's right."

"Why don't you borrow my old Winchester?"

"You think I might need it?"

Buck winked. "You've made some people here mighty unhappy and you're going off by yourself. Besides that, you might come across a couple of rattlesnakes."

"I wouldn't kill them with a rifle."

Buck thought about that for a moment and then he smiled and said, "You're absolutely right, Marshal. What you need is to borrow my big old double-barreled shotgun. Sometimes those rattlers run in packs . . . if you catch my drift."

"Buck, I think you've got something there. Thanks."

Twenty minutes later, Longarm was driving a small, flat-bedded wagon through the town and then turning north on the road that followed the river. When he'd ridden the blue roan he'd made far better time but the horse Buck had hitched to the wagon was a short but chunky sorrel mare that was steady and moved along at a slow but even pace. She had the smallest, cutest ears Longarm had ever seen on a horse and she flicked them back and forth with every stride.

When he came in sight of the NO TRESPASSING! sign, Longarm stopped and examined the shotgun. Satisfied and with a half-dozen extra shotgun shells in his pockets, he drove on toward the gold mine.

"Hold up there!" a stranger shouted, grabbing a Winchester and coming forward. "This here property is off limits to everyone but those that own it or work it."

Longarm looked past the man toward the mine, eyes searching for Albert or Carl but not seeing either man. "I came looking for a couple of your workers, mister. No need to point that rifle at me."

"Who the hell are you?" The rifleman was almost dancing with excitement. "You be a lawman from Denver!"

It came to Longarm in a flash. This man was newly hired and he'd been warned to shoot on sight . . . especially if the intruder was a federal marshal from Denver."

"No, sir."

"Then state your name and your business!"

Longarm mustered up a disarming smile. "Well, I came to sell you some whiskey."

"You got whiskey?"

"I do." He glanced over his shoulder.

The man lowered the rifle a bit and started to move around so that he could see into the back of the wagon. In the brief instant when he was looking where he shouldn't, Longarm's hand flashed across his waist and out came his Colt in one smooth motion. The rifleman tried to turn and fire but he was too late. Longarm whipped his gun across his body and fired, striking the man in the forehead and blowing a hole out the back of his skull.

A moment later, two others burst out of the mine. When they saw Longarm jumping off the wagon and grabbing the Winchester, they both made a dive for the rifles resting just inside the mine. Longarm opened fire, levering the rifle as fast as he could, and the pair went down kicking. Longarm ran over to their sides and saw that one was dead, the other was shot in the gut.

"Where are Albert Dodd and Carl Wittman!" he yelled, kneeling beside the dying man. "Where are they, damn you!"

The miner looked up at Longarm and a bloody froth came out of his mouth when he hissed, "We killed them turncoat sons o' bitches! Shot and dragged their bodies out into the river and let 'em sink for the catfish to eat."

Longarm sagged with defeat. The eyes of the man began to glaze over with death and Longarm knew he'd heard the truth.

Their witnesses were dead. And now, not even Judge Peter Hamilton was going to declare that Tom Ray had acted in self-defense.

Longarm was furious not only with the three killers he'd just shot but with himself for not coming sooner to collect the two critical witnesses. Now what in the hell were they going to do?

In his fury, Longarm was not inclined to load the three bodies onto the rented wagon and take them back to town. There would be many questions to answer and it would only complicate an already impossible situation.

He paced back and forth in front of the mine for several minutes as flies buzzed overhead and the short, sorrel mare flicked her eyes rapidly to keep them off her face. He looked at the last wheelbarrow load of rocks that had been taken from the mine and studied them for flecks of gold and found none. He then went to a small tailings pile and studied the most recent rock that had come out of the mine and found that it was almost devoid of quartz.

"They've run out of gold and the mine isn't producing much if anything anymore," he said to himself.

But what to do now?

Stopping, he saw a couple of sticks of dynamite and reached a quick decision. With sweat pouring down his face, he dragged all three bodies all the way back into the mine then hurried outside and grabbed two sticks of dynamite. He wrapped their long fuses together and lit them then ran about ten feet into the mine and hurled them back into the darkness.

Toward the three bodies. He whirled and raced outside and he didn't stop or slow down until he had a good hold on the mare.

The explosion was muffled but a storm-like cloud of rock dust belched from the mouth of the cave, and the sorrel mare backed up in terror.

"It's all right," he told the frightened animal. "It'll just be the two of us heading back to Yuma. Soon, you'll be back in your barn and I'll be trying to figure out what I'm going to do next."

Longarm climbed back onto the wagon and studied the scene. The camp was littered with empty cans and bottles. He could smell man shit and the flies were thick and menacing. But just a short ways away the Colorado River rolled on, brown with silt, but placid and with a touch of sunlight dancing on its ripples. And somewhere under that deceptively slow surface two bodies were bouncing along on the riverbed headed toward the Gulf of Mexico. Maybe they were just now passing Prison Hill.

It all made a man wonder.

"Let's go," Longarm told the mare as he turned the wagon back toward Yuma, trying to imagine how he was going to break this terrible news to Jessica, Kent, and Peter Hamilton.

Chapter 22

They were crowded into Kent and Jessica's hotel room, heads bent in thought, saying nothing in response to the news that their two key witnesses were now fish bait. Finally, Longarm said, "Albert and Carl were good, simple miners. I really feel bad for what happened to them and know they didn't deserve their sad fates."

Judge Peter Hamilton came to his feet. "You didn't say what happened to the three men that were at the mine when you arrived."

"They're gone."

The brothers looked at him for an explanation, but Longarm wasn't about to tell them that story. These men were judges and they operated strictly by the letter of the law. Telling them that he'd had to kill three more men was just going to make things even more difficult for everyone. Besides, those three had intended to kill him but he'd just gotten the job done a little quicker.

"So where are we now with a new trial?" Jessica asked.

"We can't give up and allow my father to rot on Prison Hill! He's thin and he's aging fast. And all the while they're taking a fortune in gold out of our mine!"

"No, they're not," Longarm said, surprising everyone. "I walked clear into the mine and the quartz and gold has run out . . . or very nearly so. The vein that they were working has gone dry. My hunch is that they were just taking out enough to pay expenses."

Jessica let out a wail. "Then everything is gone!"

"It always happens," Kent said quietly. "You know that gold veins peter out sooner or later."

"But . . . but that means that everything that has happened to my father has been for nothing!"

"Not so," Longarm told her. "I'm sure that Mitch Lang, the marshal, and the judge profited greatly from the gold they extracted before the vein ran out. They have stolen from you and your father and they're going to have to pay."

"How?" Jessica looked to all of them. "How can we know how much gold they took out of our mine before it went bust?"

No one had an answer to her question, but Longarm said, "Let's set a figure."

"You can't do that," Peter told him.

"Oh," Longarm said, "I think we could safely say that they took out at least twenty-five thousand dollars . . . or should we make it fifty?"

The brothers stared at him as if he might have gone daft. Longarm didn't care. It had been a bad day and he was ready to have a little fun. "I think it ought to be fifty thousand and that being the case I'm going to retrieve that much value in money, property, or whatever from those three thieves and murderers."

"Now wait just a minute," Peter cautioned. "You can't just confiscate their bank accounts and property."

"Sure, I can. But I'll wait until after you've sent them up to Prison Hill or I've sent them to hell."

No one said a word but just kept staring. Finally, Longarm barked a laugh. "Stop looking like we're finished and they've won. Jessica, the night that your father had to draw his gun and kill those two men cheating him at cards there had to be at least a few people who saw what was going on and could offer testimony if they weren't afraid of being killed."

"That's true," Kent said. "But I asked everyone and nobody would admit to seeing exactly what happened before the gunfight."

"Well," Longarm told them, "I'm going to start asking the same question all over again and I'm going to find a witness or witnesses who will testify in Tom Ray's behalf. In fact, I'm going over to the Cactus Saloon and start asking questions right now."

"I should go with you," Kent said.

"No," Longarm told him. "You and your brother lock your doors and don't let anyone in before I return. You have guns and you all know how to use them so I think you'll be fine. Oh, and don't show your lamp-lit faces in the window in case there is already a newly hired marksman sitting on some rooftop across the street."

"Okay," the brothers said. "But be careful out there. You're as much of a target as we are."

"Probably even more, if I may flatter myself," Longarm said with a grin.

The Cactus Saloon was busy, and Longarm ordered a beer and stayed at the bar just watching. The crowd was having a good time, and there were three reasonably attractive whores working on the floor and taking men out the back door on a regular basis, probably to some shack or room off the alley.

"Marshal, you are very good for my business," the bartender said. "Your beer is on the house."

"Thanks. Why am I good for business?"

"Because a lot of people here no longer have to worry about making a monthly payment in order to stay in business, myself included."

Longarm nodded with understanding. "Those deputies must have been collecting a lot of money every month."

"More than you can even imagine," the bartender said. "I owned this place for six years before Marshal Beeson and his hired guns arrived and made a deal with the devil to run Yuma."

"The devil being Mitch Lang."

The bartender and owner threw up both hands palms forward. "I didn't say that. I didn't say that at all."

"You didn't need to," Longarm told the man as he quaffed down his beer. "But I'll still take you up on a the free beer."

"As many as you want, Marshal."

Longarm leaned his elbows on the bar and watched the people, wondering which of them might have witnessed the gunfight that sent Tom Ray to Prison Hill. His eyes came to rest on one of the "working girls" who had reddish hair and the vestiges of a black eye.

"Who is that?" he asked when the bartender laid him a fresh beer down.

"That would be Loretta. She's been a steady here for almost a year."

"Someone really popped her in the eye."

"Marshal Beeson did that," the bartender said quietly.

"That big bastard is rough on the girls. It's gotten so that they aren't willing to service him anymore but he can be very persuasive so sometimes they have no choice. I pity them for having to lay down for the pig."

Longarm watched Loretta circulate the room and he noticed that she was trying to hide the fact that she was limping. "She hurt her leg?"

"After the marshal beat hell out of her, two men raped her in an alley and left her for dead."

"Were they ever arrested and brought to justice?"

The bartender shook his head. "Loretta admits she was very drunk when it happened and says that she can't remember her attacker's faces."

"Do you believe her?"

The bartender shrugged. "What does it matter? If she does know who did it, she would be in danger of being killed. She's a whore, Marshal, so what good would it do her to press charges? Judge Thompson would toss her charges in the trash can and she would be run out of town."

"Might be a good thing for her," Longarm mused. "Do you think that Loretta was here the night that Tom Ray shot those two crooked gamblers to death?"

"Where else would she be working at night?"

Longarm took a deep swallow of beer and then began to make his way toward Loretta before some man grabbed and led her out the back door.

"Hello there," he said, smiling.

Loretta was in the middle of a laugh but when she turned and saw Longarm the laughter died in her throat. Longarm saw that the bruises around her eyes were dark and swollen but the woman was still young and attractive. She had eyes that reflected considerable intelligence and sorrow.

Loretta swallowed hard and managed a professional smile. "Are you talking to *me*?"

"I am."

Loretta shook her head and looked away. "I know who you are and I'd rather not associate with you, Marshal Long."

"Sorry to hear that. I really would like to buy you a drink."

"Why?"

Longarm took her arm and led her off to one side. "I want to talk to you, Loretta."

"How do you know my name?"

"I know lots about you," Longarm said bluntly. "I know who gave you those shiners and what happened to you in an alley. And I'm wondering if you'd like me to deliver a little overdue justice in your behalf."

She pulled away from him. "What happened . . . happened. I don't want any more trouble from them or you."

"Just point your two attackers out to me if they're here," Longarm said. "That's all you have to do."

"Why should I risk getting my neck wrung?"

"Because those kinds of men will do what they did to you or another girl again and again. And maybe the next victim will die."

Loretta swallowed hard. "It was dark in the alley and I was naked and drunk."

"So I've heard." Longarm leaned close. "Tell me if they're here and don't look their way but describe them. I'll see that you get some revenge and that they don't do that to another woman . . . ever."

"You going to kill them?"

"I don't know yet, but I'm going to hurt them as bad as they hurt you."

Loretta's face suddenly twisted with anger. Tears bled from her eyes and ran freely down her cheeks. "They're standing at the bar together. One is big in a red shirt and gray Stetson, the other is smaller wearing a derby with a duck's feather sticking out of the hatband."

"That's all I need."

"Thank you, but . . ."

"Don't worry, they'll never know," Longarm promised. "But I have to have something in return."

She sniffled and wiped her cheeks dry. "I should have known. Okay, if you hurt them I'll pleasure you in whatever way you choose. If you want me right now, then let's go out the back. I'll give you the best you ever got from a whore."

"I'm sure I'd like that but I can't take you up on the offer," Longarm told her. "What I need from you is honesty."

"Honesty?"

"Yes. Can you be honest with me, Loretta?"

"If you promise to kill or at least beat up those bastards like I heard you did with the deputies, then yes, I'll be honest."

"Did you see the two men that Tom Ray shot to death in this saloon pull their guns first?"

All the color—and there wasn't much—drained out of Loretta's face and she tried to pull away but Longarm grabbed her with an iron fist. "It was self-defense, Loretta. If you saw it, then I really need you to testify in the new trial."

She looked at him as if he were insane. "Before Judge Thompson?"

"No, before a new judge who will give Tom Ray a fair trial."

"Oh my gawd, I'm going to be killed for sure!"

"I promise you I'll take care of you and protect you like

you were my own sister. And after your testimony, I'll get you out of this shithole town and take you to Denver and help find you a decent, respectable job and a place to live."

"Don't promise me things you can't deliver, Marshal. Men have been promising me things they couldn't deliver my entire life."

"I give you my word of honor. If you saw the shooting and will testify that Tom Ray fired in self-defense and that the men were cheating him at cards, then I'll help you get a new life."

"Maybe I don't deserve a new life."

"Everyone deserves a second chance. The trouble is that real second chances often come just once in a lifetime. Are you ready for yours?"

Loretta was shaking now. "Marshal, I saw the whole thing. It *was* self-defense and I knew those men were cheating Tom at cards. And . . . and I'll testify if you swear you'll help me start over."

"Deal," Longarm whispered. "Now move away from me and stay away until I've gotten you some restitution."

"Yes, sir!"

And then she was gone. Back among the crowd laughing and touching and it wasn't five minutes later that he saw her being led out the back door.

Chapter 23

Loretta's two rapists and attackers ran out of beer money and staggered out the door of the Cactus Saloon about eleven o'clock. They were drunk and weaving as Longarm closed in on them from behind. He waited until they were about to pass a dark alley and then he pounced, rushing forward to grab both men by the collars and hurl them into the alley.

Longarm hit the big man in the red shirt first and broke his nose. When he grabbed it, Longarm stepped back and kicked him as hard as he could deep up between his legs. The big man screamed and Longarm turned his attention on the smaller man, who was trying to get out of the alley and run away.

"Who are you?" the man cried.

"I'm the one that's going to give you the worst beating of your miserable life."

"No! Please!"

But after just having seen the damage these two had inflicted on Loretta's formerly pretty face, Longarm had no

pity for either of these men. He went after the smaller one
with both fists and when the man started to crumple, Longarm hurled him up against a wall and kept pounding him until
he was unrecognizable.

The bigger man was climbing to his feet when Longarm
turned around. He had a large knife in his fist and started lurch-
ing forward. Longarm crouched and when the big man made
a clumsy stabbing motion, Longarm grabbed the man's wrist,
twisted the knife around, and drove it into his opponent's groin.

"Ahhhh!"

Longarm twisted the knife in the hope of castrating this
man or at least slicing off his penis. Maybe he did, maybe
not. Either way, the large man in the red shirt was never
going to fully be a man again.

Looking down at him, Longarm said, "If you can crawl,
you might want to get back into the street before you bleed
out. Doesn't matter to me."

"Who are you!"

"I'm retribution," Longarm replied before he hurled the
bloody-bladed knife into the darkness and walked away.

Longarm washed the blood off his hands in a horse
trough and reentered the Cactus Saloon, then sought out
Loretta. She looked at him and then his hands and whispered, "Are they dead?"

"No, but they wish they were."

Loretta smiled and led him off to the side of the room
where they could talk in private and the noise wasn't quite
so loud. "Marshal, I'd like to go somewhere and be alone
with you now."

"And leave all these paying customers? I don't pay a
woman . . . ever."

"I don't want your money. You promised you were going

to give me a second chance if I testified and I will testify. All I'm asking is that my second chance begins tonight."

Longarm smiled. "You will have to make some big changes, Loretta. How old are you?"

"Twenty-three."

"All right," Longarm said. "We'll go back to my hotel and the first thing you'll do is take a long, hot bath."

"Tub big enough for both of us?" she asked.

"Just might be. And after your bath you can sleep in my room."

"In your bed . . . with you?" she asked, leaning close.

She smelled of tobacco, sweat, beer, and rough men. "Loretta, ask me that question later tonight."

"Oh, I'll ask all right. And I'll keep askin' until you give me the answer I want to hear."

Longarm understood and so he took her by the arm and guided her out of the saloon and, hopefully, into a new and far better and longer future.

Once back at the hotel, Longarm led Loretta up the stairs to his room. "I'm going to go down to the end of the hallway," he said, "and draw you a hot bath."

She looked around at his room. "This hotel doesn't allow women like me up in these rooms. The people who work here know who I am and they may . . ."

"I'll explain that you are no longer working saloons. That you've become a respectable woman."

"They won't believe that!"

Longarm shrugged. "It doesn't matter what they believe anymore. It's what *you* believe that counts."

Again, he started to leave but she grabbed his arm. "Are you sure that I won't get killed for testifying?"

"Loretta, we both know that there's nothing sure or certain in this life staying on this floor. But I can promise you that there are three other people besides me who are willing to risk our lives to right the wrong that was done to Tom Ray and to the people of Yuma."

"Is she next door with Mr. Hamilton?"

"You mean Mrs. Jessica Hamilton?"

"Yes."

"She is," Longarm said.

"I heard that she was shot and nearly killed."

"That's true, but she's doing much better now. She, her husband, and her husband's brother are all in the rooms on this floor, and tomorrow we are going to set the wheels in motion to give Tom Ray a new trial. He'll have Peter Hamilton on the bench and new jurors. And, Loretta, we'll have your sworn testimony that Tom Ray acted strictly in self-defense."

"Mr. Lang and the marshal aren't going to let this happen," Loretta said quietly. "They won't . . ."

Longarm placed a finger over her lips. "You need a bath. There's soap and shampoo for your hair. After that you ought to get a good night's sleep. I know that you're hurt and tired and frightened. But tomorrow the sun will shine, we'll get a new trial under way, and you'll give your testimony before the week is out. Then, we'll all leave this town on the train."

"Mr. Hamilton and his bride are leaving Yuma with us?"

"Yes, along with the federal judge. They've decided to relocate to Santa Fe where their parents live and need assistance."

Loretta nodded. "I heard that Santa Fe is a real nice place to live."

"So have I," Longarm told her. "And we can stay over a night or two, and if you decide you'd rather live there than in Denver, that will be fine."

But Loretta shook her head. "I want to get as far away from all this and my past as I can. I'm sticking with you."

"That'll be fine."

"Are you married?"

He almost smiled. "No."

"Engaged or have a sweetheart in Denver?"

Longarm shook his head.

"Then for sure I'm sticking with you. Marshal, if . . . if I got cleaned, I would look respectable and men used to say I was really pretty."

"I believe that."

Loretta kissed his mouth and then she headed for the door. "Do I turn right or left?"

"Right." Longarm took her arm and unlocked his door. He was still wearing his gun . . . just in case. "But I'm going with you. From now until the trial is over, you're not leaving my sight."

Her eyebrows lifted. "So are you going to sit on the shitter and watch while I take my bath?"

Longarm thought about that a moment. "It's a real big bathtub, Loretta. I might just join you."

She winked and gave her hips a little shake and bump, "Now we're talking!"

They were both laughing as they made their way down the carpeted hallway.

Chapter 24

It didn't take long for federal judge Peter Hamilton to open court with a new trial for Tom Ray, and everyone wanted to be on the new jury because this was just about the most exciting event in the history of Yuma. Now, it was one o'clock in the afternoon. Tom Ray was in court dressed in his prison clothes and guarded by a pair of very serious guards armed with shotguns. No one expected the prisoner to try to escape but there was a sense of danger in the air and the warden himself had promised to appear later in the afternoon.

A short time earlier Tom Ray had stated once again the circumstances that night when he'd been playing poker in the Cactus Saloon. Having been a United States marshal out of Denver for many years, he was very familiar with court proceedings and gave a creditable testimony. Even more in his favor was the fact that he had been well liked in the community while the two crooked gamblers had been feared and despised.

Much to her anger and frustration, Dr. Kelly had refused to allow Jessica to attend the retrial, and Longarm was glad. He had hired a tough pair of men to guard her hotel room door with strict orders not to let anyone inside except himself, the doctor, and her husband.

"This will all be over by the end of the day," Kent Hamilton told his wife just before leaving. "Everyone knows that Lang and the marshal stole your mine and plundered it of gold these past several months. There isn't even going to be a prosecuting attorney in attendance."

"Hopefully," Jessica said, "when everyone hears Loretta's sworn testimony, there will be a quick 'not guilty' verdict and my father will be with us tonight."

"That's the way we see it," Kent said, glancing at Longarm, who nodded in agreement. "And as soon as he's free, I'm going to ask the court to take a look at how much the gold was worth that was taken from your mine. We'll get a quick settlement that will set us up with a new house in Santa Fe."

"Are you just going to abandon our Yuma house?" Jessica asked.

"I found someone who will sell it and everything in it. He's getting a commission based on the sale money."

"But . . ."

"Don't worry about it," Kent said. "Until I got you for my bride, I didn't have a damn thing worth keeping. We'll make a fresh start and start with new things that we find together."

"I'd like that very much," Jessica told him.

"Me, too. When we leave with the money we'll get from the court . . . and I'm hoping it will be at least twenty thousand . . . I can open an office in Santa Fe and with my brother's connections I'll prosper."

"I don't care about having a lot of money," Jessica said. "But to be honest, I never wanted to be poor, either."

Kent laughed. "We're going to do just fine once this trial is over and your father is free. You don't think he'll want to stick around Yuma, do you?"

"My father has a mind all of his own and he'll usually do what is unexpected. But I think he's seen enough of this country to last him the rest of his lifetime. And he once told me that he loved Santa Fe because it's much cooler in the summer and the winters aren't harsh."

"I hope he comes and lives with us."

"He won't," Jessica said with confidence. "Tom will come to Santa Fe and then he'll be off looking for the end of the rainbow."

"Maybe he'll find a pretty senorita instead."

"I sure hope so."

Jessica kissed her husband and then for good measure she kissed Longarm and Loretta. "You two are risking your lives today to help my father and that is something Kent and I will never forget."

"Justice is its own best reward," Longarm replied.

"Loretta . . . I can't thank you enough. You're being very brave to take the stand."

"I'll tell nothing but the truth and when this is over, I'll start a new life with Custis in Denver."

Jessica's eyebrows lifted in surprise and she stared at Longarm. "Is that right?"

"I'm just going to help her get a fresh start, so don't let your imagination start getting the best of you."

Longarm knew what she was thinking but decided to just let it pass. Sure, Loretta had been a whore and probably had sex with more men in a month than he'd had in his life, but her slate was going to be swept clean and after a bath and with her hair brushed, she was looking very good. The pair of eye shiners were growing fainter every day and she wasn't even limping anymore. Yeah, he'd be proud to put her on his arm and walk her down Colfax Avenue, and maybe she could even teach him a few new tricks on the train heading back to Colorado and later on in his bed.

"Be careful," Jessica warned. "Be very, very careful. Mitch Lang has something planned and—"

"We'll be careful," Longarm interrupted. "Just rest easy and don't worry. The two men I hired are very capable and they won't run out on you if there is trouble."

"All right," Jessica said. "Good-bye and good luck. I can't wait to see and hold my father once more."

"Are you both ready?" Longarm asked Kent and the visibly frightened Loretta as they descended the stairway into the lobby.

"Ready as could be," Kent said tightly.

"Me, too," Loretta whispered, "Custis, just stay real close."

"I will."

Monty waved from behind the hotel desk. "Good luck, Marshal! The whole town is cheering for Tom Ray!"

"Thanks," Longarm called as they headed outside and walked across the street, heading for the courthouse, which was only a block away.

"Just relax," Longarm said, feeling how tight Loretta's arm felt against his own. "This won't take long and once you've testified, you won't be in any danger at—"

The shot from the rooftop punched a round, neat hole through Longarm's hat brim and blasted dirt into the air. An instant later, Longarm hurled Loretta behind a horse-watering trough and dove in after her. Jessica's husband landed tight against them as more rifle shots boomed.

"Someone is on the roof!" Longarm growled.

"I caught a glimpse of his face. It's Marshal Beeson," Kent whispered. "What are we going to do?"

"You and Loretta are going to stay where you are. I'm going after him. Don't move until I call out that this is finished and you're no longer in any danger."

Two more rifle shots riddled the wooden trough and twin streams of water began to pour over their heads. Longarm drew his pistol and poked his head over the trough bringing another fast bullet that narrowly missed.

"He won't stay up there," Longarm decided. "Beeson is on the bank's rooftop, and now that he realizes he's missed his best chance of killing me and Loretta, he'll be running."

"Be careful!" Loretta whispered.

Longarm wasn't listening but instead was rolling fast toward the sidewalk, and when he was out of Beeson's rifle sights, he burst into the bank and shouted, "Is there a stairway to the rooftop!"

There were two people in the bank and one of them was Mitch Lang. Longarm just caught a glimpse of the banker as he scuttled out of sight and then there was the crashing sound of a door slamming from the back of the building.

Longarm jumped over a desk and went after the crooked banker. He found the back door to the bank and kicked it open yelling, "It's over, Lang! Same for you, Beeson!"

He heard the pounding of feet across the bank's rooftop. Longarm looked around and then spied a rusty ladder attached to the building. He began to climb, knowing that if the marshal of the banker were thinking straight, they would have hurried over to shoot directly downward at him. His heart was pounding and it seemed to take forever to reach the rooftop, but he rolled over the edge, yanking out his pistol.

The rooftop was empty but Longarm saw empty shell casings from a Winchester, and when he rushed to the far edge of the rooftop, he caught a glimpse of Marshal Beeson and Mitch Lang sprinting down a back alley. Lang was the faster and smaller man, but the heavyset marshal was close on his heels. Having no clear shot, Longarm watched them disappear.

He drew a deep breath and holstered his gun. He had a choice to make . . . he could either chase after the pair or he could make sure that Loretta was safe and able to testify in court.

Take care of Loretta, he thought. *Then after her testimony go after those two. You gave everyone your word you'd protect them and that, along with seeing Tom Ray go free, is the most important thing you can do now.*

Longarm climbed back down the bank's ladder and slapped rust from the palms of his hands. He hurried around the building to see Loretta and Kent still lying flat on their bellies with twin streams of water still pouring over them.

"It's okay to come out now," he yelled as he trotted over to join the pair.

Kent helped Loretta up and they were both covered with mud.

"I can't go into the courtroom looking like this!" Kent complained, furiously wiping his face and the front of his coat and pants but only making things look worse.

"And I don't want anyone to see me on the stand looking so awful!" Loretta wailed.

Longarm understood. But sometimes you had to do what you didn't want to do and this was one of those times.

"Here," he said, pulling out his handkerchief and dipping it in the water trough. "Wipe the mud off your faces and let's get over to that courthouse. Justice for Tom Ray can't wait until we look respectable."

"Easy for you to say," Loretta told him as she smeared mud across her pretty face while scrubbing furiously. "You're a man!"

Longarm didn't understand what being a man or a woman had to do with having a muddy face and clothes, but he decided he had more than enough on his mind already so he let the remark pass.

Despite the years of being mistreated and humiliated, Loretta still had a bit of a defiant streak in her because she placed both of her muddy thumbs on Longarm's cheeks and drew a couple of lines that looked like Comanche war paint.

"There," she said, looking satisfied, "we'll *all* look the same now."

"Okay by me," Longarm said, taking her hand and heading for the courtroom.

Chapter 25

Finally, the trial was almost over. Judge Peter Hamilton, the Yuma jury, and dozens of spectators had packed the baking courtroom and intently listened to a muddy-faced but determined Loretta describe how Tom Ray had acted in self-defense.

"They drew first and they were cheating him and that pair of poor miners," she said. "In my opinion, Mr. Tom Ray should have been awarded a *medal* instead of sent to prison."

Everyone nodded in agreement, mopping their sweaty faces. Tom Ray was smiling from ear to ear and that smile stayed plastered to his face when federal judge Peter Hamilton said, "Has the jury reached a verdict?"

"Not guilty!" all the jurors shouted.

"Then by the authority given to me by the United States of America I declare you, Tom Ray, absolved off all charges and a free man!"

The packed courthouse erupted in cheers and a woman with a face flushed by the heat fainted dead away. Everyone

cleared out fast and Longarm stood back to watch the pair
of prison guards unshackle the man and shake his hand.
Kent Hamilton hugged his brother and then his new father-
in-law.

"I want to see Jessica! I want to see my girl!" Tom Ray
shouted.

"We're going to her right now," her husband yelled as he
led the newly freed man out of the courtroom.

For a full minute, Tom Ray just stood on the front steps
of the courthouse smiling and breathing in the hot and
free air.

"I want my gold mine back," he said to Kent.

"Of course, but it has run dry."

Ray frowned. "Are you sure of that?"

"Yes, sir. But we're going to attach one hell of a lot of
assets from Mitch Lang to make up for the gold that was
plundered. I promise you'll be satisfied before this is all said
and done."

Tom Ray nodded. "Then I take you at your promise.
Truth of the matter is that I was dreading working that
damned old mine again and I'm sure that now that Jessica
has married you she wouldn't have been too keen on
helping."

"Probably not," Kent said, trying to hide a smile. "Come
on. She's waiting upstairs in the hotel."

Longarm had taken Loretta back to their room and kissed
her good-bye. He'd shaken hands with everyone and it did
his heart proud to see how happy the former Denver lawman was to be with his daughter again, even if she was
wounded.

"Loretta," Longarm said, "I have to be after them before
they get too great a lead on me."

"Please . . ."

"You're going to tell me to be careful."

"Yes! I want to make love to you when you return . . . if you think I'm worthy of doing it . . . I mean, given my past and . . ."

Longarm put his fingers over her mouth. "I'll be back and we'll make love. That's a promise."

She hugged him so tightly that she nearly broke his neck and then Longarm was flying down the stairs.

"Git them bastards!" Monty shouted from behind the hotel's registration desk.

"I'll do my best," Longarm yelled back over his shoulder.

Now Longarm was mounting a horse at the Rolling River Stables and the owner was handing him a rifle. "Marshal, you need to just kill 'em both! Don't just arrest 'em and bring 'em back to be tried by a jury. Mr. Lang has enough money to buy the best lawyers in the land and they might get him off the hook."

"I'm a federal officer sworn to uphold the law, not to execute people no matter how much they deserve it."

"I know," the liveryman conceded. "But if Mitch Lang . . . with all his money and influence . . . ever gets a toehold back in this town, anyone who stood against him this day will be ruthlessly killed or destroyed. You understand what I'm saying?"

"I completely understand," Longarm told the man. "Thanks for the loan of the rifle and the ammunition."

"Use it all up on them two bastards! Don't waste a single bullet."

"I'll do my best."

The liveryman patted the horse he'd selected for Longarm.

"This paint is the fastest and toughest animal I ever owned. He won't quit on you and he'll run until he drops."

"Thanks."

Longarm was eager to get into the saddle and head out after Lang and Beeson, but the liveryman really wanted to talk.

"Marshal, I was in the courtroom today and when I heard those shots outside from the rooftop, I just knew that you and Loretta were dead. Then, when the three of you marched in with mud all over your faces and clothes . . . I couldn't believe my eyes. Neither could anyone else. That's when everyone started yelling and stomping and shouting in celebration."

"I'll have to admit it was quite a boisterous reception," Longarm agreed.

"Marshal, my guess is that they headed across the river and hope to overtake the westbound train for San Diego," the liveryman said. "It went through here right after the shooting and if they catch it you may never capture them two evil sons o' bitches."

"I'll catch them no matter how far or fast they run."

"Just be careful crossing the Colorado River. There's a place about a quarter mile north of the train trestle and it's where people cross when they have to get into California. The water is going to be high and dangerous, but this pony you're taking can damn sure swim. Go to that place if you need to cross over."

"Thanks for the warning. Where is the next train stop rolling west from here?"

"That would be Holtville and I never been there and I'd guess it would be about sixty miles . . . but all desert and it's just a whistle stop where they take on water and wood."

"Well," Longarm said, "I sure hope I don't have to ride that far after those two."

"Here, take a couple of extra canteens." The liveryman ran into a tack room and hurried back with two large canteens. "Fill 'em up when you're crossin' the river and don't let that fine horse I'm lending you get bit by a snake or his wind broken plowing through them gawdamn California sand dunes."

"I won't."

"Shoot them on sight, Marshal. Because if they spot you first, you can damn sure betcha that's what they'll do!"

Longarm nodded with understanding and rode out of the stable and through town. He saw Loretta standing on the courthouse steps surrounded by newfound friends and they all waved. Loretta called out something to him but Longarm couldn't hear her words over the hard pounding of his horse's shod hooves.

Beeson and Lang had crossed the river into California, probably by running on foot over the train trestle and then finding horses to buy or rent. Longarm made the river crossing where he'd been told, but once in California he had to spend ten or fifteen minutes before anyone could actually point him in the direction that the Yuma fugitives had taken. Lang and Beeson had not dared to cross the desert and reach Holtville. Instead, they'd galloped south crossing an unmarked border into old Mexico and staying close to the west bank of the Colorado River. Their tracks were very fresh and Longarm knew that he could overtake them before it got dark.

At sundown he saw Lang and Beeson less than a mile up ahead, and when they finally realized Longarm was closing in, they tried to cross the river again. But down in Mexico, the farmers had already siphoned off a lot of the river onto their carefully tended fields and now the Colorado was shallow and treacherous with sandbars.

Longarm wasn't yet in rifle range when he saw Lang's horse flounder in quicksand. The man shouted a warning to Beeson, but it was too late. Both horses quickly sank to their bellies, wildly pawing and fighting for a footing not to be found. But the animals sank only so far and then they were stuck, unable to move except for their heads, which they kept waving helplessly. Longarm knew that by tomorrow some Mexican farmer would see the trapped saddled horses. He would round up more men and some mules and ropes. And in a short time, the two mired-down saddle horses would be pulled free and some poor Mexican peasant would have been gifted beyond his wildest dreams.

Longarm rode to the very edge of the muddy, slow-moving river fully aware that he had no authority in Mexico to exact American justice. Down here below the border it was every man for himself.

Longarm dragged the Winchester out of his saddle scabbard. He tied his fine horse and walked a few dozen yards south along the bank so that any shots fired back at him would not hit his pinto. He saw a fish jump into the sunset and splash a miniature golden rainbow.

Longarm stretched out on the warm Mexican sand and used his thumb to ease his ruined hat back just a little on his sweating forehead. The sun was to his back, diving into the western hills. His targets were to the east and now abandoning their poor horses while trying to escape to the opposite shore.

Longarm watched the two Yuma men struggle and

decided not to give them the chance to reach the opposite riverbank. They were both fighting the quicksand and he could hear their anguished grunting over the sounds of evening birds flitting through the sage and water-loving cottonwood trees.

The pair were exhausted from the struggles and made very easy targets.

Longarm rested his rifle on a sun-bleached log, settled into the warm sand, and took careful aim.

He didn't waste any ammunition because he didn't miss.

GIANT-SIZED ADVENTURE FROM AVENGING ANGEL LONGARM.

BY TABOR EVANS

penguin.com/actionwesterns

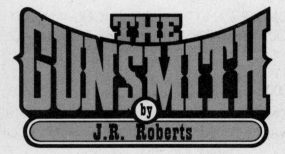